DATE DUE	
~~APR 2 6 2010~~		

Gorilla,
My
Love

Gorilla, My Love

BY

TONI CADE BAMBARA

Vintage Books
A Division of Random House
New York

"Sweet Town" first appeared in Vendome, January, 1959.
"Mississippi Ham Rider" first appeared in The Massachusetts
Review, Summer 1960; also appeared in Black and White in
American Culture, University of Massachusetts Press, 1969.
"The Hammer Man" first appeared in Negro Digest, February,
1966; also appeared in What's Happening, Scott Foresman
& Co., 1969. "Playin With Punjab" first apppeared in
Liberator Magazine, February, 1967. "Talkin Bout Sonny"
first apeared in Liberator Magazine, June, 1967. "Maggie
of the Green Bottles" first appeared in Prairie Schooner
Magazine, Winter 1967/68. "Happy Birthday" first appeared
in What's Happening, Scott, Foresman, 1969. "Blues Ain't
No Mockin Bird" first appeared in Another I/Eye, Scott,
Foresman, 1971; also appeared in Redbook Magazine,
April 1972. "Raymond's Run" first appeared in Tales and
Short Stories for Black Folks, Doubleday, 1971; also appeared
in Redbook Magazine, June, 1971. "My Man Bovanne" first
appeared in Black World, October, 1971, under the title
"Mamma Hazel Takes to Her Bed." "Gorilla, My Love" first
appeared in Redbook Magazine, November, 1971, under the
title "I Ain't Playin, I'm Hurtin."

Library of Congress Cataloging in Publication Data
Bambara, Toni Cade.
Gorilla, my love.
Reprint. Originally published: New York:
Random House, 1972.
I. Title.
PS3552.A473G6 1981   813'.54   81-3013
ISBN 0-394-75049-7   AACR2

Manufactured in the United States of America

9

To the Johnson Girls
with the deepest and most compassionate
love and respect

A
Sort
of
Preface

It does no good to write autobiographical fiction cause the minute the book hits the stand here comes your mama screamin how could you and sighin death where is thy sting and she snatches you up out your bed to grill you about what was going down back there in Brooklyn when she was working three jobs and trying to improve the quality of your life and come to find on page 42 that you were messin around with that nasty boy up the block and breaks into sobs and quite naturally your family strolls in all sleepy-eyed to catch the floor show at 5:00 A.M. but as far as your mama is concerned, it is nineteen-forty-and-something and you ain't too grown to have your ass whipped.

And it's no use using bits and snatches even of real events and real people, even if you do cover, guise, switch-around and change-up cause next thing you know your best friend's laundry cart is squeaking past but your bell ain't ringing so you trot down the block after her and there's this drafty cold pressure front the weatherman surely did not predict and your friend says in this chilly way that it's really something when your own friend stabs you in the back with a pen and for the next two blocks you try to explain that the character is not her at all but just happens to be speaking one of her lines and right about the time you hit the laundromat and you're ready to just give it up and take the weight, she turns to you and says that seeing as how you have plundered her soul and walked off with a piece of her flesh, the least you can do is spin off half the royalties her way.

So I deal in straight-up fiction myself, cause I value my family and friends, and mostly cause I lie a lot anyway.

Contents

A Sort of Preface   ix

My Man Bovanne   1

Gorilla, My Love   11

Raymond's Run   21

The Hammer Man   33

Mississippi Ham Rider   45

Happy Birthday   59

Playin With Punjab   67

Talkin Bout Sonny   77

The Lesson   85

The Survivor   97

Sweet Town   119

Blues Ain't No Mockin Bird   127

Basement   137

Maggie of the Green Bottles   149

The Johnson Girls   161

My Man Bovanne

*B*LIND PEOPLE got a hummin jones if you notice. Which is understandable completely once you been around one and notice what no eyes will force you into to see people, and you get past the first time, which seems to come out of nowhere, and it's like you in church again with fat-chest ladies and old gents gruntin a hum low in the throat to whatever the preacher be saying. Shakey Bee bottom lip all swole up with Sweet Peach and me explainin how come the sweet-potato bread was a dollar-quarter this time stead of dollar regular and he say uh hunh he understand, then he break into this *thizzin* kind of hum which is quiet, but fiercesome just the same, if you ain't ready for it. Which I wasn't. But I got used to it and the onliest time I had to say somethin bout it was when he was playin checkers on the stoop one time and he commenst to hummin quite churchy seem to me. So I says, "Look here Shakey Bee, I can't beat you and Jesus too." He stop.

So that's how come I asked My Man Bovanne to dance. He ain't my man mind you, just a nice ole gent from the block that we all know cause he fixes things and the kids like him. Or used to fore Black Power got hold their minds and mess em around till they can't be civil to ole folks. So we at this

3

benefit for my niece's cousin who's runnin for somethin with this Black party somethin or other behind her. And I press up close to dance with Bovanne who blind and I'm hummin and he hummin, chest to chest like talkin. Not jammin my breasts into the man. Wasn't bout tits. Was bout vibrations. And he dug it and asked me what color dress I had on and how my hair was fixed and how I was doin without a man, not nosy but nice-like, and who was at this affair and was the canapés dainty-stingy or healthy enough to get hold of proper. Comfy and cheery is what I'm tryin to get across. Touch talkin like the heel of the hand on the tambourine or on a drum.

But right away Joe Lee come up on us and frown for dancin so close to the man. My own son who knows what kind of warm I am about; and don't grown men call me long distance and in the middle of the night for a little Mama comfort? But he frown. Which ain't right since Bovanne can't see and defend himself. Just a nice old man who fixes toasters and busted irons and bicycles and things and changes the lock on my door when my men friends get messy. Nice man. Which is not why they invited him. Grass roots you see. Me and Sister Taylor and the woman who does heads at Mamies and the man from the barber shop, we all there on account of we grass roots. And I ain't never been souther than Brooklyn Battery and no more country than the window box on my fire escape. And just yesterday my kids tellin me to take them countrified rags off my head and be cool. And now can't get Black enough to suit em. So everybody passin sayin My Man Bovanne. Big deal, keep steppin and don't even stop a minute to get the man a drink or one of them cute sandwiches or tell him what's goin on. And him standin there with a smile ready case someone do speak he want to be ready. So that's how come I pull him on the dance floor and we dance squeezin past the tables and chairs and all them coats and people standin round up in each other face talkin bout this and that but got no use for this blind man who mostly fixed skates and skooters for all these folks when they was just kids. So I'm pressed up close and we touch talkin with the hum. And here come my daughter cuttin her eye at me like she do when she tell me about my "apolitical" self like I got hoof and mouf disease and there ain't no hope at all. And I don't pay her no mind and just look up in Bovanne shadow face and tell him his stomach like a drum and he laugh. Laugh real loud. And here come my youngest, Task, with a tap on my elbow like he the third grade monitor and I'm cuttin up on the line to assembly.

"I was just talkin on the drums," I explained when they hauled me into the kitchen. I figured drums was my best defense. They can get ready for drums what with all this heritage business. And Bovanne stomach just like that drum Task give me when he come back from Africa. You just touch it and it hum thizzm, thizzm. So I stuck to the drum story. "Just drummin that's all."

"Mama, what are you talkin about?"

"She had too much to drink," say Elo to Task cause she don't hardly say nuthin to me direct no more since that ugly argument about my wigs.

"Look here Mama," say Task, the gentle one. "We just tryin to pull your coat. You were makin a spectacle of yourself out there dancing like that."

"Dancin like what?"

Task run a hand over his left ear like his father for the world and his father before that.

"Like a bitch in heat," say Elo.

"Well uhh, I was goin to say like one of them sex-starved ladies gettin on in years and not too discriminating. Know what I mean?"

I don't answer cause I'll cry. Terrible thing when your own children talk to you like that. Pullin me out the party and hustlin me into some stranger's kitchen in the back of a bar just like the damn police. And ain't like I'm old old. I can still wear me some sleeveless dresses without the meat hangin off my arm. And I keep up with some thangs through my kids. Who ain't kids no more. To hear them tell it. So I don't say nuthin.

"Dancin with that tom," say Elo to Joe Lee, who leanin on the folks' freezer. "His feet can smell a cracker a mile away and go into their shuffle number post haste. And them eyes. He could be a little considerate and put on some shades. Who wants to look into them blown-out fuses that—"

"Is this what they call the generation gap?" I say.

"Generation gap," spits Elo, like I suggested castor oil and fricassee possum in the milk-shakes or somethin. "That's a white concept for a white phenomenon. There's no generation gap among Black people. We are a col—"

"Yeh, well never mind," says Joe Lee. "The point is Mama . . . well, it's pride. You embarrass yourself and us too dancin like that."

"I wasn't shame." Then nobody say nuthin. Them standin there in they pretty clothes with drinks in they hands and gangin up on me, and me in the third-degree chair and nary a olive to my name. Felt just like the police got hold to me.

"First of all," Task say, holdin up his hand and tickin off the offenses, "the dress. Now that dress is too short, Mama, and too low-cut for a woman your age. And Tamu's going to make a speech tonight to kick off the campaign and will be introducin you and expecting you to organize the council of elders—"

"Me? Didn nobody ask me nuthin. You mean Nisi? She change her name?"

"Well, Norton was supposed to tell you about it. Nisi wants to introduce you and then encourage the older folks to form a Council of the Elders to act as an advisory—"

"And you going to be standing there with your boobs out and that wig on your head and that hem up to your ass. And

6

people'll say, 'Ain't that the horny bitch that was grindin with the blind dude?' "

"Elo, be cool a minute," say Task, gettin to the next finger. "And then there's the drinkin. Mama, you know you can't drink cause next thing you know you be laughin loud and carryin on," and he grab another finger for the loudness. "And then there's the dancin. You been tattooed on the man for four records straight and slow draggin even on the fast numbers. How you think that look for a woman your age?"

"What's my age?"

"What?"

"I'm axin you all a simple question. You keep talkin bout what's proper for a woman my age. How old am I anyhow?" And Joe Lee slams his eyes shut and squinches up his face to figure. And Task run a hand over his ear and stare into his glass like the ice cubes goin calculate for him. And Elo just starin at the top of my head like she goin rip the wig off any minute now.

"Is your hair braided up under that thing? If so, why don't you take it off? You always did do a neat cornroll."

"Uh huh," cause I'm thinkin how she couldn't undo her hair fast enough talking bout cornroll so countrified. None of which was the subject. "How old, I say?"

"Sixtee-one or—"

"You a damn lie Joe Lee Peoples."

"And that's another thing," say Task on the fingers.

"You know what you all can kiss," I say, gettin up and brushin the wrinkles out my lap.

"Oh, Mama," Elo say, puttin a hand on my shoulder like she hasn't done since she left home and the hand landin light and not sure it supposed to be there. Which hurt me to my heart. Cause this was the child in our happiness fore Mr. Peoples die. And I carried that child strapped to my chest till she was nearly two. We was close is what I'm tryin to tell you. Cause it was more me in the child than the others. And even after Task it was the girlchild I covered in the night and wept over for no reason at all less it was she was a chub-chub like me and not very pretty, but a warm child. And how did things get to this, that she can't put a sure hand on me and say Mama we love you and care about you and you entitled to enjoy yourself cause you a good woman?

"And then there's Reverend Trent," say Task, glancin from left to right like they hatchin a plot and just now lettin me in on it. "You were suppose to be talking with him tonight, Mama, about giving us his basement for campaign headquarters and—"

"Didn nobody tell me nuthin. If grass roots mean you kept in the dark I can't use it. I really can't. And Reven Trent a fool anyway the way he tore into the widow man up there on Edgecomb cause he wouldn't take in three of them foster children and the woman not even comfy in the ground yet and the man's mind messed up and—"

"Look here," say Task. "What we need is a family conference so we can get all this stuff cleared up and laid out on the table. In the meantime I think we better get back into the other room and tend to business. And in the meantime, Mama, see if you can't get to Reverend Trent and—"

"You want me to belly rub with the Reven, that it?"

"Oh damn," Elo say and go through the swingin door.

"We'll talk about all this at dinner. How's tomorrow night, Joe Lee?" While Joe Lee being self-important I'm wonderin who's doin the cookin and how come no body ax me if I'm free and do I get a corsage and things like that. Then Joe nod that it's O.K. and he go through the swingin door and just a little hubbub come through from the other room. Then Task smile his smile, lookin just like his daddy and he leave. And it just me in this stranger's kitchen, which was a mess I wouldn't never let my kitchen look like. Poison you just to look at the pots. Then the door swing the other way and it's My Man Bovanne standin there sayin Miss Hazel but lookin at the deep fry and then at the steam table, and most surprised when I come up on him from the other direction and take him on out of there. Pass the folks pushin up towards the stage where Nisi and some other people settin and ready to talk, and folks gettin to the last of the sandwiches and the booze fore they settle down in one spot and listen serious. And I'm thinkin bout tellin Bovanne what a lovely long dress Nisi got on and the earrings and her hair piled up in a cone and the people bout to hear how we all gettin screwed and gotta form our own party and everybody there listenin and lookin. But instead I just haul the man on out of there, and Joe Lee and his wife look at me like I'm terrible, but they ain't said boo to the man yet. Cause he blind and old and don't nobody there need him since they grown up and don't need they skates fixed no more.

"Where we goin, Miss Hazel?" Him knowin all the time.

"First we gonna buy you some dark sunglasses. Then you comin with me to the supermarket so I can pick up tomorrow's dinner, which is goin to be a grand thing proper and you invited. Then we goin to my house."

"That be fine. I surely would like to rest my feet." Bein cute, but you got to let men play out they little show, blind or not. So he chat on bout how tired he is and how he appreciate me takin him in hand this way. And I'm thinkin I'll have him change the lock on my door first thing. Then I'll give the man a nice warm bath with jasmine leaves in the water and a little Epsom salt on the sponge to do his back. And then a good rubdown with rose water and olive oil. Then a cup of lemon tea with a taste in it. And a little talcum, some of that fancy stuff Nisi mother sent over last Christmas. And then a massage, a good face massage round the forehead which is the worryin part. Cause you gots to take care of the older folks. And let them know they still needed to run the mimeo machine and keep the spark plugs clean and fix the mailboxes for folks who might help us get the breakfast program goin,

and the school for the little kids and the campaign and all.
Cause old folks is the nation. That what Nisi was sayin and I
mean to do my part.

"I imagine you are a very pretty woman, Miss Hazel."

"I surely am," I say just like the hussy my daughter always
say I was.

Gorilla,
My
Love

*T*HAT WAS THE YEAR Hunca Bubba changed his name. Not a change up, but a change back, since Jefferson Winston Vale was the name in the first place. Which was news to me cause he'd been my Hunca Bubba my whole lifetime, since I couldn't manage Uncle to save my life. So far as I was concerned it was a change completely to somethin soundin very geographical weatherlike to me, like somethin you'd find in a almanac. Or somethin you'd run across when you sittin in the navigator seat with a wet thumb on the map crinkly in your lap, watchin the roads and signs so when Granddaddy Vale say "Which way, Scout," you got sense enough to say take the next exit or take a left or whatever it is. Not that Scout's my name. Just the name Granddaddy call whoever sittin in the navigator seat. Which is usually me cause I don't feature sittin in the back with the pecans. Now, you figure pecans all right to be sittin with. If you thinks so, that's your business. But they dusty sometime and make you cough. And they got a way of slidin around and dippin down sudden, like maybe a rat in the buckets. So if you scary like me, you sleep with the lights on and blame it on Baby Jason and, so as not to waste good electric, you study the maps. And that's how come I'm in the navigator seat most times and get to be called Scout.

So Hunca Bubba in the back with the pecans and Baby Jason, and he in love. And we got to hear all this stuff about this woman he in love with and all. Which really ain't enough to keep the mind alive, though Baby Jason got no better sense than to give his undivided attention and keep grabbin at the photograph which is just a picture of some skinny woman in a countrified dress with her hand shot up to her face like she shame fore cameras. But there's a movie house in the background which I ax about. Cause I am a movie freak from way back, even though it do get me in trouble sometime.

Like when me and Big Brood and Baby Jason was on our own last Easter and couldn't go to the Dorset cause we'd seen all the Three Stooges they was. And the RKO Hamilton was closed readying up for the Easter Pageant that night. And the West End, the Regun and the Sunset was too far, less we had grownups with us which we didn't. So we walk up Amsterdam Avenue to the Washington and *Gorilla, My Love* playin, they say, which suit me just fine, though the "my love" part kinda drag Big Brood some. As for Baby Jason, shoot, like Granddaddy say, he'd follow me into the fiery furnace if I say come on. So we go in and get three bags of Havmore potato chips which not only are the best potato chips but the best bags for blowin up and bustin real loud so the matron come trottin down the aisle with her chunky self, flashin that flashlight dead in your eye so you can give her some lip, and if she answer back and you already finish seein the show anyway, why then you just turn the place out. Which I love to do, no lie. With Baby Jason kickin at the seat in front, egging me on, and Big Brood mumblin bout what fiercesome things we goin do. Which means me. Like when the big boys come up on us talkin bout Lemme a nickel. It's me that hide the money. Or when the bad boys in the park take Big Brood's Spaudeen way from him. It's me that jump on they back and fight awhile. And it's me that turns out the show if the matron get too salty.

So the movie come on and right away it's this churchy music and clearly not about no gorilla. Bout Jesus. And I am ready to kill, not cause I got anything gainst Jesus. Just that when you fixed to watch a gorilla picture you don't wanna get messed around with Sunday School stuff. So I am mad. Besides, we see this raggedy old brown film *King of Kings* every year and enough's enough. Grownups figure they can treat you just anyhow. Which burns me up. There I am, my feet up and my Havmore potato chips really salty and crispy and two jawbreakers in my lap and the money safe in my shoe from the big boys, and here comes this Jesus stuff. So we all go wild. Yellin, booin, stompin and carryin on. Really to wake the man in the booth up there who musta went to sleep and put on the wrong reels. But no, cause he holler down to shut up and then he turn the sound up so we really gotta holler like crazy to even hear ourselves good. And the matron ropes off the children section and flashes her light all over the place and we yell some more and some kids slip under the rope and run up and down the aisle just to show it take more than some dusty ole velvet rope to tie us down. And I'm flingin the kid in front of me's popcorn. And Baby Jason kickin seats. And it's really somethin. Then here come the big and bad matron, the one they let out in case of emergency. And she totin that flashlight like she gonna use it on somebody. This here the colored matron Brandy and her friends call Thunderbuns. She do not play. She do not smile. So we shut up and watch the simple ass picture.

Which is not so simple as it is stupid. Cause I realize that just about anybody in my family is better than this god they always talkin about. My daddy wouldn't stand for nobody treatin any of us that way. My mama specially. And I can just see it now, Big Brood up there on the cross talkin bout Forgive them Daddy cause they don't know what they doin. And my Mama say Get on down from there you big fool, whatcha think this is, playtime? And my Daddy yellin to Granddaddy to get him a ladder cause Big Brood actin the fool, his mother side of the family showin up. And my mama and her sister Daisy jumpin on them Romans beatin them with they pocketbooks. And Hunca Bubba tellin them folks on they knees they better get out the way and go get some help or they goin to get trampled on. And Granddaddy Vale sayin Leave the boy alone, if that's what he wants to do with his life we ain't got nothin to say about it. Then Aunt Daisy givin him a taste of that pocketbook, fussin bout what a damn fool old man Granddaddy is. Then everybody jumpin in his chest like the time Uncle Clayton went in the army and come back with only one leg and Granddaddy say somethin stupid about that's life. And by this time Big Brood off the cross and in the park playin handball or skully or somethin. And the family in the kitchen throwin dishes at each other, screamin bout if you hadn't done this I wouldn't had to do that. And me in the parlor trying to do my arithmetic yellin Shut it off.

Which is what I was yellin all by myself which make me a sittin target for Thunderbuns. But when I yell We want our money back, that gets everybody in chorus. And the movie windin up with this heavenly cloud music and the smart-ass up there in his hole in the wall turns up the sound again to drown us out. Then there comes Bugs Bunny which we already seen so we know we been had. No gorilla my nuthin. And Big Brood say Awwww sheeet, we goin to see the manager and get our money back. And I know from this we business. So I brush the potato chips out of my hair which is where Baby Jason like to put em, and I march myself up the aisle to deal with the manager who is a crook in the first place for lyin out there sayin *Gorilla, My Love* playin. And I never did like the man cause he oily and pasty at the same time like the bad guy in the serial, the one that got a hideout behind

a push-button bookcase and play "Moonlight Sonata" with
gloves on. I knock on the door and I am furious. And I am
alone, too. Cause Big Brood suddenly got to go so bad even
though my mama told us bout goin in them nasty bathrooms.
And I hear him sigh like he disgusted when he get to the door
and see only a little kid there. And now I'm really furious
cause I get so tired grownups messin over kids just cause they
little and can't take em to court. What is it, he say to me like
I lost my mittens or wet on myself or am somebody's re-
tarded child. When in reality I am the smartest kid P.S. 186
ever had in its whole lifetime and you can ax anybody. Even
them teachers that don't like me cause I won't sing them
Southern songs or back off when they tell me my questions
are out of order. And cause my Mama come up there in a
minute when them teachers start playin the dozens behind
colored folks. She stalk in with her hat pulled down bad and
that Persian lamb coat draped back over one hip on account
of she got her fist planted there so she can talk that talk which
gets us all hypnotized, and teacher be comin undone cause
she know this could be her job and her behind cause Mama
got pull with the Board and bad by her own self anyhow.

So I kick the door open wider and just walk right by him
and sit down and tell the man about himself and that I want
my money back and that goes for Baby Jason and Big Brood
too. And he still trying to shuffle me out the door even though
I'm sittin which shows him for the fool he is. Just like them
teachers do fore they realize Mama like a stone on that spot
and ain't backin up. So he ain't gettin up off the money. So
I was forced to leave, takin the matches from under his ashtray, and set a fire under the candy stand, which closed the
raggedy ole Washington down for a week. My Daddy had the
suspect it was me cause Big Brood got a big mouth. But I
explained right quick what the whole thing was about and I
figured it was even-steven. Cause if you say Gorilla, My Love,
you suppose to mean it. Just like when you say you goin to

give me a party on my birthday, you gotta mean it. And if you
say me and Baby Jason can go South pecan haulin with
Granddaddy Vale, you better not be comin up with no stuff
about the weather look uncertain or did you mop the bathroom or any other trickified business. I mean even gangsters
in the movies say My word is my bond. So don't nobody get
away with nothin far as I'm concerned. So Daddy put his belt
back on. Cause that's the way I was raised. Like my Mama
say in one of them situations when I won't back down, Okay
Badbird, you right. Your point is well-taken. Not that Badbird
my name, just what she say when she tired arguin and know
I'm right. And Aunt Jo, who is the hardest head in the family
and worse even than Aunt Daisy, she say, You absolutely
right Miss Muffin, which also ain't my real name but the
name she gave me one time when I got some medicine shot
in my behind and wouldn't get up off her pillows for nothin.
And even Granddaddy Vale—who got no memory to speak
of, so sometime you can just plain lie to him, if you want to
be like that—he say, Well if that's what I said, then that's it.
But this name business was different they said. It wasn't like
Hunca Bubba had gone back on his word or anything. Just
that he was thinkin bout gettin married and was usin his real
name now. Which ain't the way I saw it at all.

So there I am in the navigator seat. And I turn to him and
just plain ole ax him. I mean I come right on out with it. No
sense goin all around that barn the old folks talk about. And
like my mama say, Hazel—which is my real name and what
she remembers to call me when she bein serious—when you
got somethin on your mind, speak up and let the chips fall
where they may. And if anybody don't like it, tell em to come
see your mama. And Daddy look up from the paper and say,
You hear your mama good, Hazel. And tell em to come see
me first. Like that. That's how I was raised.

So I turn clear round in the navigator seat and say, "Look

here, Hunca Bubba or Jefferson Windsong Vale or whatever
your name is, you gonna marry this girl?"

"Sure am," he say, all grins.

And I say, "Member that time you was baby-sittin me
when we lived at four-o-nine and there was this big snow and
Mama and Daddy got held up in the country so you had to
stay for two days?"

And he say, "Sure do."

"Well. You remember how you told me I was the cutest
thing that ever walked the earth?"

"Oh, you were real cute when you were little," he say,
which is suppose to be funny. I am not laughin.

"Well. You remember what you said?"

And Grandaddy Vale squintin over the wheel and axin
Which way, Scout. But Scout is busy and don't care if we all
get lost for days.

"Watcha mean, Peaches?"

"My name is Hazel. And what I mean is you said you were
going to marry *me* when I grew up. You were going to wait.
That's what I mean, my dear Uncle Jefferson." And he don't
say nuthin. Just look at me real strange like he never saw me
before in life. Like he lost in some weird town in the middle
of night and lookin for directions and there's no one to ask.
Like it was me that messed up the maps and turned the road
posts round. "Well, you said it, didn't you?" And Baby Jason
lookin back and forth like we playin ping-pong. Only I ain't
playin. I'm hurtin and I can hear that I am screamin. And
Grandaddy Vale mumblin how we never gonna get to where
we goin if I don't turn around and take my navigator job
serious.

"Well, for cryin out loud, Hazel, you just a little girl. And
I was just teasin."

" 'And I was just teasin,' " I say back just how he said it so
he can hear what a terrible thing it is. Then I don't say

nuthin. And he don't say nuthin. And Baby Jason don't say nuthin nohow. Then Granddaddy Vale speak up. "Look here, Precious, it was Hunca Bubba what told you them things. This here, Jefferson Winston Vale." And Hunca Bubba say, "That's right. That was somebody else. I'm a new somebody."

"You a lyin dawg," I say, when I meant to say treacherous dog, but just couldn't get hold of the word. It slipped away from me. And I'm crying and crumplin down in the seat and just don't care. And Granddaddy say to hush and steps on the gas. And I'm losin my bearins and don't even know where to look on the map cause I can't see for cryin. And Baby Jason cryin too. Cause he is my blood brother and understands that we must stick together or be forever lost, what with grown-ups playin change-up and turnin you round every which way so bad. And don't even say they sorry.

Raymond's
Run

I DON'T HAVE MUCH WORK to do around the house like some girls. My mother does that. And I don't have to earn my pocket money by hustling; George runs errands for the big boys and sells Christmas cards. And anything else that's got to get done, my father does. All I have to do in life is mind my brother Raymond, which is enough.

Sometimes I slip and say my little brother Raymond. But as any fool can see he's much bigger and he's older too. But a lot of people call him my little brother cause he needs looking after cause he's not quite right. And a lot of smart mouths got lots to say about that too, especially when George was minding him. But now, if anybody has anything to say to Raymond, anything to say about his big head, they have to come by me. And I don't play the dozens or believe in standing around with somebody in my face doing a lot of talking. I much rather just knock you down and take my chances even if I am a little girl with skinny arms and a squeaky voice, which is how I got the name Squeaky. And if things get too rough, I run. And as anybody can tell you, I'm the fastest thing on two feet.

There is no track meet that I don't win the first place medal. I used to win the twenty-yard dash when I was a little kid in kindergarten. Nowadays, it's the fifty-yard dash. And tomorrow I'm subject to run the quarter-meter relay all by myself and come in first, second, and third. The big kids call me Mercury cause I'm the swiftest thing in the neighborhood. Everybody knows that—except two people who know better, my father and me. He can beat me to Amsterdam Avenue with me having a two fire-hydrant headstart and him running with his hands in his pockets and whistling. But that's private information. Cause can you imagine some thirty-five-year-old man stuffing himself into PAL shorts to race little kids? So as far as everyone's concerned, I'm the fastest and that goes for Gretchen, too, who has put out the tale that she is going to win the first-place medal this year. Ridiculous. In the second place, she's got short legs. In the third place, she's got freckles. In the first place, no one can beat me and that's all there is to it.

I'm standing on the corner admiring the weather and about to take a stroll down Broadway so I can practice my breathing exercises, and I've got Raymond walking on the inside close to the buildings, cause he's subject to fits of fantasy and starts thinking he's a circus performer and that the curb is a tightrope strung high in the air. And sometimes after a rain he likes to step down off his tightrope right into the gutter and slosh around getting his shoes and cuffs wet. Then I get hit when I get home. Or sometimes if you don't watch him he'll dash across traffic to the island in the middle of Broadway and give the pigeons a fit. Then I have to go behind him apologizing to all the old people sitting around trying to get some sun and getting all upset with the pigeons fluttering around them, scattering their newspapers and upsetting the waxpaper lunches in their laps. So I keep Raymond on the inside of me, and he plays like he's driving a stage coach which is O.K. by me so long as he doesn't run me over or interrupt my breathing exercises, which I have to do on account of I'm serious about my running, and I don't care who knows it.

Now some people like to act like things come easy to them, won't let on that they practice. Not me. I'll high-prance down 34th Street like a rodeo pony to keep my knees strong even if it does get my mother uptight so that she walks ahead like she's not with me, don't know me, is all by herself on a shopping trip, and I am somebody else's crazy child. Now you take Cynthia Procter for instance. She's just the opposite. If there's a test tomorrow, she'll say something like, "Oh, I guess I'll play handball this afternoon and watch television tonight," just to let you know she ain't thinking about the test. Or like last week when she won the spelling bee for the millionth time, "A good thing you got 'receive,' Squeaky, cause I would have got it wrong. I completely forgot about the spelling bee." And she'll clutch the lace on her blouse like it was a narrow escape. Oh, brother. But of course when I pass her house on my early morning trots around the block, she is practicing the scales on the piano over and over and over and over. Then in music class she always lets herself get bumped around so she falls accidently on purpose onto the piano stool and is so surprised to find herself sitting there that she decides just for fun to try out the ole keys. And what do you know—Chopin's waltzes just spring out of her finger-tips and she's the most surprised thing in the world. A regular prodigy. I could kill people like that. I stay up all night study-ing the words for the spelling bee. And you can see me any time of day practicing running. I never walk if I can trot, and shame on Raymond if he can't keep up. But of course he does, cause if he hangs back someone's liable to walk up to him and get smart, or take his allowance from him, or ask him where he got that great big pumpkin head. People are so stupid sometimes.

So I'm strolling down Broadway breathing out and breathing in on counts of seven, which is my lucky number, and here comes Gretchen and her sidekicks: Mary Louise, who used to be a friend of mine when she first moved to

Harlem from Baltimore and got beat up by everybody till I took up for her on account of her mother and my mother used to sing in the same choir when they were young girls, but people ain't grateful, so now she hangs out with the new girl Gretchen and talks about me like a dog; and Rosie, who is as fat as I am skinny and has a big mouth where Raymond is concerned and is too stupid to know that there is not a big deal of difference between herself and Raymond and that she can't afford to throw stones. So they are steady coming up Broadway and I see right away that it's going to be one of those Dodge City scenes cause the street ain't that big and they're close to the buildings just as we are. First I think I'll step into the candy store and look over the new comics and let them pass. But that's chicken and I've got a reputation to consider. So then I think I'll just walk straight on through them or even over them if necessary. But as they get to me, they slow down. I'm ready to fight, cause like I said I don't feature a whole lot of chit-chat, I much prefer to just knock you down right from the jump and save everybody a lotta precious time.

"You signing up for the May Day races?" smiles Mary Louise, only it's not a smile at all. A dumb question like that doesn't deserve an answer. Besides, there's just me and Gretchen standing there really, so no use wasting my breath talking to shadows.

"I don't think you're going to win this time," says Rosie, trying to signify with her hands on her hips all salty, completely forgetting that I have whupped her behind many times for less salt than that.

"I always win cause I'm the best," I say straight at Gretchen who is, as far as I'm concerned, the only one talking in this ventriloquist-dummy routine. Gretchen smiles, but it's not a smile, and I'm thinking that girls never really smile at each other because they don't know how and don't want to know how and there's probably no one to teach us how, cause grown-up girls don't know either. Then they all look at Raymond who has just brought his mule team to a standstill. And they're about to see what trouble they can get into through him.

"What grade you in now, Raymond?"

"You got anything to say to my brother, you say it to me, Mary Louise Williams of Raggedy Town, Baltimore."

"What are you, his mother?" sasses Rosie.

"That's right, Fatso. And the next word out of anybody and I'll be *their* mother too." So they just stand there and Gretchen shifts from one leg to the other and so do they. Then Gretchen puts her hands on her hips and is about to say something with her freckle-face self but doesn't. Then she walks around me looking me up and down but keeps walking up Broadway, and her sidekicks follow her. So me and Raymond smile at each other and he says, "Gidyap" to his team and I continue with my breathing exercises, strolling down Broadway toward the ice man on 145th with not a care in the world cause I am Miss Quicksilver herself.

I take my time getting to the park on May Day because the track meet is the last thing on the program. The biggest thing on the program is the May Pole dancing, which I can do without, thank you, even if my mother thinks it's a shame I don't take part and act like a girl for a change. You'd think my mother'd be grateful not to have to make me a white organdy dress with a big satin sash and buy me new white baby-doll shoes that can't be taken out of the box till the big day. You'd think she'd be glad her daughter ain't out there prancing around a May Pole getting the new clothes all dirty and sweaty and trying to act like a fairy or a flower or whatever you're supposed to be when you should be trying to be yourself, whatever that is, which is, as far as I am concerned, a poor Black girl who really can't afford to buy shoes and a new dress you only wear once a lifetime cause it won't fit next year.

27

I was once a strawberry in a Hansel and Gretel pageant when I was in nursery school and didn't have no better sense than to dance on tiptoe with my arms in a circle over my head doing umbrella steps and being a perfect fool just so my mother and father could come dressed up and clap. You'd think they'd know better than to encourage that kind of nonsense. I am not a strawberry. I do not dance on my toes. I run. That is what I am all about. So I always come late to the May Day program, just in time to get my number pinned on and lay in the grass till they announce the fifty-yard dash.

I put Raymond in the little swings, which is a tight squeeze this year and will be impossible next year. Then I look around for Mr. Pearson, who pins the numbers on. I'm really looking for Gretchen if you want to know the truth, but she's not around. The park is jam-packed. Parents in hats and corsages and breast-pocket handkerchiefs peeking up. Kids in white dresses and light-blue suits. The parkees unfolding chairs and chasing the rowdy kids from Lenox as if they had no right to be there. The big guys with their caps on backwards, leaning against the fence swirling the basketballs on the tips of their fingers, waiting for all these crazy people to clear out the park so they can play. Most of the kids in my class are carrying bass drums and glockenspiels and flutes. You'd think they'd put in a few bongos or something for real like that.

Then here comes Mr. Pearson with his clipboard and his cards and pencils and whistles and safety pins and fifty million other things he's always dropping all over the place with his clumsy self. He sticks out in a crowd because he's on stilts. We used to call him Jack and the Beanstalk to get him mad. But I'm the only one that can outrun him and get away, and I'm too grown for that silliness now.

"Well, Squeaky," he says, checking my name off the list and handing me number seven and two pins. And I'm thinking he's got no right to call me Squeaky, if I can't call him Beanstalk.

"Hazel Elizabeth Deborah Parker," I correct him and tell him to write it down on his board.

"Well, Hazel Elizabeth Deborah Parker, going to give someone else a break this year?" I squint at him real hard to see if he is seriously thinking I should lose the race on purpose just to give someone else a break. "Only six girls running this time," he continues, shaking his head sadly like it's my fault all of New York didn't turn out in sneakers. "That new girl should give you a run for your money." He looks around the park for Gretchen like a periscope in a submarine movie. "Wouldn't it be a nice gesture if you were . . . to ahhh . . ."

I give him such a look he couldn't finish putting that idea into words. Grownups got a lot of nerve sometimes. I pin number seven to myself and stomp away, I'm so burnt. And I go straight for the track and stretch out on the grass while the band winds up with "Oh, the Monkey Wrapped His Tail Around the Flag Pole," which my teacher calls by some other name. The man on the loudspeaker is calling everyone over to the track and I'm on my back looking at the sky, trying to pretend I'm in the country, but I can't, because even grass in the city feels hard as sidewalk, and there's just no pretending you are anywhere but in a "concrete jungle" as my grandfather says.

The twenty-yard dash takes all of two minutes cause most of the little kids don't know no better than to run off the track or run the wrong way or run smack into the fence and fall down and cry. One little kid, though, has got the good sense to run straight for the white ribbon up ahead so he wins. Then the second-graders line up for the thirty-yard dash and I don't even bother to turn my head to watch cause Raphael Perez always wins. He wins before he even begins by psyching the runners, telling them they're going to trip on their shoelaces and fall on their faces or lose their shorts or something, which he doesn't really have to do since he is very fast, almost as fast as I am. After that is the forty-yard dash which I use to run when I was in first grade. Raymond is hollering from the swings cause he knows I'm about to do my thing cause the man on the loudspeaker has just announced the fifty-yard dash, although he might just as well be giving a recipe for angel food cake cause you can hardly make out what he's sayin for the static. I get up and slip off my sweat pants and then I see Gretchen standing at the starting line, kicking her legs out like a pro. Then as I get into place I see that ole Raymond is on line on the other side of the fence, bending down with his fingers on the ground just like he knew what he was doing. I was going to yell at him but then I didn't. It burns up your energy to holler.

Every time, just before I take off in a race, I always feel like I'm in a dream, the kind of dream you have when you're sick with fever and feel all hot and weightless. I dream I'm flying over a sandy beach in the early morning sun, kissing the leaves of the trees as I fly by. And there's always the smell of apples, just like in the country when I was little and used to think I was a choo-choo train, running through the fields of corn and chugging up the hill to the orchard. And all the time I'm dreaming this, I get lighter and lighter until I'm flying over the beach again, getting blown through the sky like a feather that weighs nothing at all. But once I spread my fingers in the dirt and crouch over the Get on Your Mark, the dream goes and I am solid again and am telling myself, Squeaky you must win, you must win, you are the fastest thing in the world, you can even beat your father up Amsterdam if you really try. And then I feel my weight coming back just behind my knees then down to my feet then into the earth and the pistol shot explodes in my blood and I am off and weightless again, flying past the other runners, my arms pumping up and down and the whole world is quiet except for the crunch as I zoom over the gravel in the track. I glance

to my left and there is no one. To the right, a blurred
Gretchen, who's got her chin jutting out as if it would win the
race all by itself. And on the other side of the fence is Raymond with his arms down to his side and the palms tucked
up behind him, running in his very own style, and it's the first
time I ever saw that and I almost stop to watch my brother
Raymond on his first run. But the white ribbon is bouncing
toward me and I tear past it, racing into the distance till my
feet with a mind of their own start digging up footfuls of dirt
and brake me short. Then all the kids standing on the side
pile on me, banging me on the back and slapping my head
with their May Day programs, for I have won again and
everybody on 151st Street can walk tall for another year.

"In first place . . ." the man on the loudspeaker is clear as
a bell now. But then he pauses and the loudspeaker starts to
whine. Then static. And I lean down to catch my breath and
here comes Gretchen walking back, for she's overshot the
finish line too, huffing and puffing with her hands on her hips
taking it slow, breathing in steady time like a real pro and I
sort of like her a little for the first time. "In first place . . ."
and then three or four voices get all mixed up on the loudspeaker and I dig my sneaker into the grass and stare at
Gretchen who's staring back, we both wondering just who
did win. I can hear old Beanstalk arguing with the man on
the loudspeaker and then a few others running their mouths
about what the stopwatches say. Then I hear Raymond yanking at the fence to call me and I wave to shush him, but he
keeps rattling the fence like a gorilla in a cage like in them
gorilla movies, but then like a dancer or something he starts
climbing up nice and easy but very fast. And it occurs to me,
watching how smoothly he climbs hand over hand and
remembering how he looked running with his arms down to
his side and with the wind pulling his mouth back and his
teeth showing and all, it occurred to me that Raymond would
make a very fine runner. Doesn't he always keep up with me

on my trots? And he surely knows how to breathe in counts of seven cause he's always doing it at the dinner table, which drives my brother George up the wall. And I'm smiling to beat the band cause if I've lost this race, or if me and Gretchen tied, or even if I've won, I can always retire as a runner and begin a whole new career as a coach with Raymond as my champion. After all, with a little more study I can beat Cynthia and her phony self at the spelling bee. And if I bugged my mother, I could get piano lessons and become a star. And I have a big rep as the baddest thing around. And I've got a roomful of ribbons and medals and awards. But what has Raymond got to call his own?

So I stand there with my new plans, laughing out loud by this time as Raymond jumps down from the fence and runs over with his teeth showing and his arms down to the side, which no one before him has quite mastered as a running style. And by the time he comes over I'm jumping up and down so glad to see him—my brother Raymond, a great runner in the family tradition. But of course everyone thinks I'm jumping up and down because the men on the loud-speaker have finally gotten themselves together and compared notes and are announcing "In first place—Miss Hazel Elizabeth Deborah Parker." (Dig that.) "In second place—Miss Gretchen P. Lewis." And I look over at Gretchen wondering what the "P" stands for. And I smile. Cause she's good, no doubt about it. Maybe she'd like to help me coach Raymond; she obviously is serious about running, as any fool can see. And she nods to congratulate me and then she smiles. And I smile. We stand there with this big smile of respect between us. It's about as real a smile as girls can do for each other, considering we don't practice real smiling every day, you know, cause maybe we too busy being flowers or fairies or strawberries instead of something honest and worthy of respect . . . you know . . . like being people.

The
Hammer
Man

I WAS GLAD TO HEAR that Manny had fallen off the roof. I had put out the tale that I was down with yellow fever, but nobody paid me no mind, least of all Dirty Red who stomped right in to announce that Manny had fallen off the roof and that I could come out of hiding now. My mother dropped what she was doing, which was the laundry, and got the whole story out of Red. "Bad enough you gots to hang around with boys," she said. "But fight with them too. And you would pick the craziest one at that."

Manny was supposed to be crazy. That was his story. To say you were bad put some people off. But to say you were crazy, well, you were officially not to be messed with. So that was his story. On the other hand, after I called him what I called him and said a few choice things about his mother, his face did go through some piercing changes. And I did kind of wonder if maybe he sure was nuts. I didn't wait to find out. I got in the wind. And then he waited for me on my stoop all day and all night, not hardly speaking to the people going in and out. And he was there all day Saturday, with his sister bringing him peanut-butter sandwiches and cream sodas. He must've gone to the bathroom right there cause every time I looked out the kitchen window, there he was. And Sunday, too. I got to thinking the boy was mad.

"You got no sense of humor, that's your trouble," I told him. He looked up, but he didn't say nothing. All at once I was real sorry about the whole thing. I should've settled for hitting off the little girls in the school yard, or waiting for Frankie to come in so we could raise some kind of hell. This way I had to play sick when my mother was around cause my father had already taken away my BB gun and hid it.

I don't know how they got Manny on the roof finally. Maybe the Wakefield kids, the ones who keep the pigeons, called him up. Manny was a sucker for sick animals and things like that. Or maybe Frankie got some nasty girls to go up on the roof with him and got Manny to join him. I don't know. Anyway, the catwalk had lost all its cement and the roof always did kind of slant downward. So Manny fell off the roof. I got over my yellow fever right quick, needless to say, and ventured outside. But by this time I had already told Miss Rose that Crazy Manny was after me. And Miss Rose, being who she was, quite naturally went over to Manny's house and said a few harsh words to his mother, who, being who she was, chased Miss Rose out into the street and they commenced to get with it, snatching bottles out of the garbage cans and breaking them on the johnny pumps and stuff like that.

Dirty Red didn't have to tell us about this. Everybody could see and hear all. I never figured the garbage cans for an arsenal, but Miss Rose came up with sticks and table legs and things, and Manny's mother had her share of scissor blades and bicycle chains. They got to rolling in the streets and all you could see was pink drawers and fat legs. It was something else. Miss Rose is nutty but Manny's mother's crazier than Manny. They were at it a couple of times during my sick spell. Everyone would congregate on the window sills or the fire escape, commenting that it was still much too cold for this kind of nonsense. But they watched anyway. And then Manny fell off the roof. And that was that. Miss Rose went back to her dream books and Manny's mother went back to her tumbled-down kitchen of dirty clothes and bundles and bundles of rags and children.

My father got in on it too, cause he happened to ask Manny one night why he was sitting on the stoop like that every night. Manny told him right off that he was going to kill me first chance he got. Quite naturally this made my father a little warm, me being his only daughter and planning to become a doctor and take care of him in his old age. So he had a few words with Manny first, and then he got hold of the older brother, Bernard, who was more his size. Bernard didn't see how any of it was his business or my father's business, so my father got mad and jammed Bernard's head into the mailbox. Then my father started getting messages from Bernard's uncle about where to meet him for a show-down and all. My father didn't say a word to my mother all this time; just sat around mumbling and picking up the phone and putting it down, or grabbing my stickball bat and putting it back. He carried on like this for days till I thought I would scream if the yellow fever didn't have me so weak. And then Manny fell off the roof, and my father went back to his beer-drinking buddies.

I was in the school yard, pitching pennies with the little boys from the elementary school, when my friend Violet hits my brand-new Spaudeen over the wall. She came running back to tell me that Manny was coming down the block. I peeked beyond the fence and there he was all right. He had his head all wound up like a mummy and his arm in a sling and his leg in a cast. It looked phony to me, especially that walking cane. I figured Dirty Red had told me a tale just to get me out there so Manny could stomp me, and Manny was playing it up with costume and all till he could get me.

"What happened to him?" Violet's sisters whispered. But I was too busy trying to figure out how this act was supposed to work. Then Manny passed real close to the fence and gave me a look.

"You had enough, Hammer Head," I yelled. "Just bring your crummy self in this yard and I'll pick up where I left off." Violet was knocked out and the other kids went into a huddle. I didn't have to say anything else. And when they all pressed me later, I just said, "You know that hammer he always carries in his fatigues?" And they'd all nod waiting for the rest of a long story. "Well, I took it away from him." And I walked off nonchalantly.

Manny stayed indoors for a long time. I almost forgot about him. New kids moved into the block and I got all caught up with that. And then Miss Rose finally hit the numbers and started ordering a whole lot of stuff through the mail and we would sit on the curb and watch these weird-looking packages being carried in, trying to figure out what simple-minded thing she had thrown her money away on when she might just as well wait for the warm weather and throw a block party for all her godchildren.

After a while a center opened up and my mother said she'd increase my allowance if I went and joined because I'd have to get out of my pants and stay in skirts, on account of that's the way things were at the center. So I joined and got to thinking about everything else but old Hammer Head. It was a rough place to get along in, the center, but my mother said that I needed to be be'd with and she needed to not be with me, so I went. And that time I sneaked into the office, that's when I really got turned on. I looked into one of those not-quite-white folders and saw that I was from a deviant family in a deviant neighborhood. I showed my mother the word in the dictionary, but she didn't pay me no mind. It was my favorite word after that. I ran it in the ground till one day my father got the strap just to show how deviant he could get.

So I gave up trying to improve my vocabulary. And I almost gave up my dungarees.

Then one night I'm walking past the Douglas Street park cause I got thrown out of the center for playing pool when I should've been sewing, even though I had already decided that this was going to be my last fling with boy things, and starting tomorrow I was going to fix my hair right and wear skirts all the time just so my mother would stop talking about her gray hairs, and Miss Rose would stop calling me by my brother's name by mistake. So I'm walking past the park and there's ole Manny on the basketball court, perfecting his lay-ups and talking with himself. Being me, I quite naturally walk right up and ask what the hell he's doing playing in the dark, and he looks up and all around like the dark had crept up on him when he wasn't looking. So I knew right away that he'd been out there for a long time with his eyes just going along with the program.

"There was two seconds to go and we were one point behind," he said, shaking his head and staring at his sneakers like they was somebody. "And I was in the clear. I'd left the men in the backcourt and there I was, smiling, you dig, cause it was in the bag. They passed the ball and I slid the ball up nice and easy cause there was nothing to worry about. And . . ." He shook his head. "I muffed the goddamn shot. Ball bounced off the rim . . ." He stared at his hands. "The game of the season. Last game." And then he ignored me altogether, though he wasn't talking to me in the first place. He went back to the lay-ups, always from the same spot with his arms crooked in the same way, over and over. I must've gotten hypnotized cause I probably stood there for at least an hour watching like a fool till I couldn't even see the damn ball, much less the basket. But I stood there anyway for no reason I know of. He never missed. But he cursed himself away. It was torture. And then a squad car pulled up and a short cop with hair like one of the Marx Brothers came out hitching up his pants. He looked real hard at me and then at Manny.

"What are you two doing?"

"He's doing a lay-up. I'm watching," I said with my smart self.

Then the cop just stood there and finally turned to the other one who was just getting out of the car.

"Who unlocked the gate?" the big one said.

"It's always unlocked," I said. Then we three just stood there like a bunch of penguins watching Manny go at it.

"This on the level?" the big guy asked, tilting his hat back with the thumb the way big guys do in hot weather. "Hey you," he said, walking over to Manny. "I'm talking to you." He finally grabbed the ball to get Manny's attention. But that didn't work. Manny just stood there with his arms out waiting for the pass so he could save the game. He wasn't paying no mind to the cop. So, quite naturally, when the cop slapped him upside his head it was a surprise. And when the cop started counting three to go, Manny had already recovered from the slap and was just ticking off the seconds before the buzzer sounded and all was lost.

"Gimme the ball, man." Manny's face was all tightened up and ready to pop.

"Did you hear what I said, black boy?"

Now, when somebody says that word like that, I gets warm. And crazy or no crazy, Manny was my brother at that moment and the cop was the enemy.

"You better give him back his ball," I said. "Manny don't take no mess from no cops. He ain't bothering nobody. He's gonna be Mister Basketball when he grows up. Just trying to get a little practice in before the softball season starts."

"Look here, sister, we'll run you in too," Harpo said.

"I damn sure can't be your sister seeing how I'm a black girl. Boy, I sure will be glad when you run me in so I can tell everybody about that. You must think you're in the South, mister."

The big guy screwed his mouth up and let one of them hard-day sighs. "The park's closed, little girl, so why don't you and your boyfriend go on home."

That really got me. The "little girl" was bad enough but that "boyfriend" was too much. But I kept cool, mostly because Manny looked so pitiful waiting there with his hands in a time-out and there being no one to stop the clock. But I kept my cool mostly cause of that hammer in Manny's pocket and no telling how frantic things can get what with a big-mouth like me, a couple of wise cops, and a crazy boy too.

"The gates are open," I said real quiet-like, "and this here's a free country. So why don't you give him back his ball?"

The big cop did another one of those sighs, his specialty I guess, and then he bounced the ball to Manny who went right into his gliding thing clear up to the backboard, damn near like he was some kind of very beautiful bird. And then he swooshed that ball in, even if there was no net, and you couldn't really hear the swoosh. Something happened to the bones in my chest. It was something.

"Crazy kids anyhow," the one with the wig said and turned to go. But the big guy watched Manny for a while and I guess something must've snapped in his head, cause all of a sudden he was hot for taking Manny to jail or court or somewhere and started yelling at him and everything, which is a bad thing to do to Manny, I can tell you. And I'm standing there thinking that none of my teachers, from kindergarten right on up, none of them knew what they were talking about. I'll be damned if I ever knew one of them rosy-cheeked cops that smiled and helped you get to school without neither you or your little raggedy dog getting hit by a truck that had a smile on its face, too. Not that I ever believed it. I knew Dick and Jane was full of crap from the get-go, especially them cops. Like this dude, for example, pulling on Manny's clothes like that when obviously he had just done about the most beautiful thing a man can do and not be a fag. No cop could swoosh without a net.

"Look out, man," was all Manny said, but it was the way he pushed the cop that started the real yelling and threats. And I thought to myself, Oh God here I am trying to change my ways, and not talk back in school, and do like my mother wants, but just have this last fling, and now this—getting shot in the stomach and bleeding to death in Douglas Street park and poor Manny getting pistol-whipped by those bastards and whatnot. I could see it all, practically crying too. And it just wasn't no kind of thing to happen to a small child like me with my confirmation picture in the paper next to my weeping parents and schoolmates. I could feel the blood sticking to my shirt and my eyeballs slipping away, and then that confirmation picture again; and my mother and her gray hair; and Miss Rose heading for the precinct with a shotgun; and my father getting old and feeble with no one to doctor him up and all.

And I wished Manny had fallen off the damn roof and died right then and there and saved me all this aggravation of being killed with him by these cops who surely didn't come out of no fifth-grade reader. But it didn't happen. They just took the ball and Manny followed them real quiet-like right out of the park into the dark, then into the squad car with his head drooping and his arms in a crook. And I went on home cause what the hell am I going to do on a basketball court, and it getting to be nearly midnight?

I didn't see Manny no more after he got into that squad car. But they didn't kill him after all cause Miss Rose heard he was in some kind of big house for people who lose their marbles. And then it was spring finally, and me and Violet was in this very boss fashion show at the center. And Miss Rose bought me my first corsage—yellow roses to match my shoes.

Mississippi
Ham
Rider

I'LL BE HERE TOMORROW for my early-morning coffee fix. If you gonna meet me, sister, bring your own dime." He swiveled away from the counter and stomped out past the jukebox, huddling his greatcoat around him. I flipped my notebook open and wrote: "Mississippi Ham Rider can best be described as a salty stud." We had talked for nearly an hour—or rather I had talked, he had merely rolled his eyes and stared into his cup as he swirled the watery coffee revealing the grounds—and still I had nothing to write up really except that there was no humor about the man, and, at seventy, was not particularly interested in coming to New York to cut records for the new blues series.

The waitress had wiped the counter menacingly and was leaning up against the pie display with her hands on her hips. I was trying to figure out whether I should follow Rider, put Neil on his trail, or try to scrounge up a story from the towns-folk. The waitress was tapping her foot. And the cook, a surly-looking bastard in white cap, was peeping over the edge of the kitchen counter, his head kind of cocked to the side so that the sweat beaded around his nostril. I was trying to get myself together, untangle my legs from the stool and get out of there. It was obvious that these particular sinister

folks were not going to fill my dossier with anything print-
able. I moved. But before I even reached the door I was in
the third person absentular.

"So what's this high-yaller Northern bitch doin' hittin' on
evil ole Ham?"

There was only one Rider in the ten-page directory, an
Isabele Rider, the address typed in the margin. I folded myself into Neil's Volkswagen and tried to find it. The town itself
was something out of *Alice* or Poe, the colored section was
altogether unbelievable: outhouses, corner hard-heads, a
predominance of junkyards with people in them, poverty
with all the usual trimmings. And Isabele Rider ran one of
those time-immemorial stores—love potions and dream
books and star charts and bleaching creams and depilatory
powders, and mason jars of ginger roots and cane shoots. A
girl of about sixteen was sitting on a milk box, reading a comic
book and eating a piece of sweet potato pie.

"Mrs. Isabele Rider around?" I asked.

"No." She went right on reading and eating.

"I'm Inez Williams," I said. "The people I work for are
trying to persuade Mr. Ham Rider to record some songs.
They want him to come to New York and bring his guitar.
He's a great blues singer," I said.

She looked me over and closed the book. "You want some
pie?"

"No thanks, just Mrs. Rider. She around?"

"No. Just me. I'm Melanie. My mother says Ham ain't
going nowhere, nor me either. Lady before asked me to sit-in
somewhere. My mother says I ain't going nowhere, Ham
neither."

I leaned on the counter and unbuttoned my sweater. A
badly drawn zodiac chart was right in front of me. I traced
the orbits looking for Aries the Ram to give me the high sign.
He looked like a very sick dog in the last stages of sickle-cell
anemia. I tried to figure out the best way to run it down to

this girl right quick that they didn't have to live in this town and hang around in this store and eat sweet potato pie for lunch and act like throwbacks, before I totally distracted myself with the zodiac or consideration of abnormal hemoglobins and such like.

"Look," I said, "back in the twenties a lot of record companies put out a series called race records. And a lot of blues singers and country singers and some flashy showbusiness types made a lot of records. Some made a lot of money. But when the Depression came, the companies fell apart and these singers went on home. Some stuck around and mopped floors and ran elevators. Now this jive mother who is my boss thinks he can make some bread by recording some of the old-timers. And they can make some bread too. So what I want is to get your granddaddy to come with us and sing awhile. You see?"

"You best speak to Ham himself," she said.

"I did. But he thought I was just trying to get into his business. All I do is write up a thing about the singers, about their life, and the company sticks this on the album cover."

She licked the last of the pie from her fingers and stood up. "What you wanna know?"

I whipped out my notebook. "What does he like, where does he come from, who're his friends. Stuff like that."

"We three all what's left. His landlady, Mama Teddy, looks out for him when he gets drinking and can't help himself. And I look out of his way when he gets raffish." She shrugged.

"Any chance of us all getting together? My partner, Mr. Neil McLoughlin, is the one who handles the business and all. I'd like you all to meet him."

"This some fay cat?"

"Uh . . . yeh."

49

"Uh-hunh." She ripped off the edge of the calendar and wrote an address. "This here is where we eat, Mama Teddy's. You be there at six."

Neil was going into one of his famous crouches by the time I got to the park. He had spent the day trying to find quarters for us both, which was a lost cause. There was not even a diner where we could trade notes without incident, so I fell in beside him on the bench, jostling the bottle in his pocket.

"I'm beat and burnt-out, I mean it," he wailed, rolling his eyes up to the heavens. "This is the most unfriendly town. I escaped from an unbelievable little rooming house down the road just as an incredible act of hospitality was about to be committed."

"Yeh, well, look, pull yourself together and let's deal with the Rider character first. He's quite a sketch—jackboots, the original War-One bespoke overcoat, razor scar, gravel voice and personality to match and—you ready?—he'll be damned if he's going North. Says he was badly mistreated up there. Froze his behind off one winter in Chicago. And in New York, the Negro artists had to use a drafty freight elevator to get to the recording studio."

"Not like the swell conditions here."

"He wasn't an artist here. I think the best thing to do is just tape him here and let him sign whatever release one signs."

"But old man Lyons, dearheart, wants him in the flesh to allow the poor folkway-starved sophisticates to, through a outrageous process of osmosis, which in no way should suggest miscegenation, to absorb their native—"

"All right, all right, calm down. The thing is, his last offer was to sing obscene songs for party records. He damned near committed mayhem. In short, the man don't wanna leave, buddy."

50

"But wasn't he at least knocked out by your superior charms, not to mention your long, lean gams?"

"Those are my superior and singular charms. He was totally unimpressed. But the man's seventy-something, keep in mind."

Neil slouched over into his hands. "This is hard work, I mean it. And I feel a mean and nasty spell coming on. I never had so much trouble and complication in my life before. I've got consumption of the heart and—"

"Neil, my nerves."

"They were always pretty easy to find. Mobile, Auburn, just sitting there in a beat-up room in a beat-up town in a beat-up mood, just sitting there waiting for an angel of mercy —me. Doing nothing but a moaning and a hummin' and a strummin'—"

"All right, cut it out. We're in trouble. The man don't wanna budge and all you can do is indulge in these theatrical and most unnerving, irritating fits of—"

"Dearheart, recall," he demanded, shoving his spread hand in my face. "There was old man Supper, a real nice old supper man. Kinda quiet-like and easygoing, just dipping his snuff and boiling his supper. And then ole Jug Henderson, the accident-prone saint of white lightning, fiddling away and sipping that bad stuff out of a mayonnaise jar. And—"

"Neil, my nerves."

"And ole Blind Grassy Wilson from Lynchburg, only one leg left by the time I arrived, but swinging still and real nice about talking into the machine to tell how his best gal slapped a razor across his chops."

"Enough, you're running amok." I got up and stretched my legs. "We've got to find a place called Mama Teddy's. And please, Neil, let me do the talking. I'm tired of eating sandwiches out of paper bags. Just be quiet till after we eat. And no wisecracks. We might get killed."

"Good Lord"—he jumped up—"I'm not insured. One false move and the man's liable to cut me, beat me up, starve me to death and then poison me." He grabbed himself by the throat and rolled around atop the mailbox. A truck passed, I stepped aside and acted like I wasn't with the lunatic.

"Amazing how your race has deteriorated under segregation, Neil. If only you'd had an example to follow, you might have been a halfway decent dancer."

He smoothed his hair back and walked quite business-like to the car. "Get in, woman."

Mama Teddy's was a storefront thing. Fried chicken legs and bar-b-qued ribs were painted on the window pane. And scrawled across the top of the glass in fussy little curlicues were the various price-fixed meals. In the doorway were three large jugs with soapy brown something or other in them, rag wicks stuffed into the necks and hanging over the sides to the floor. But you could see that the place was clean, sort of. I was starving. Neil was dragging along the tape recorder, mumbling statistics about hernia and prostate damage.

"You see that pickup truck over there," he whispered. "It's full of angry blacks with ugly sticks who're gonna whip my head 'cause they think you're my woman."

"Never mind, let's go find Mr. Ethnic-Authentic."

Neil tripped over the jugs and a whiff of chitlins damn near knocked me over. A greasy smell from the kitchen had jammed up my breathing before I even got into the place.

"Somebody's dying," whispered Neil.

"Soul food," I gasped, eyes watering.

"What?"

"You wouldn't understand, my boy."

The large, jovial woman who shuffled out of the kitchen with what only looked like great speed was obviously Mama Teddy. "Hi, little honey," she said, squashing me into her bosom. "Little Melanie told me all about you and you're surely welcome. You too," she said, swallowing up Neil's hand in her fist. She hustled us over to a table with cloth and flowers. "Mr. Rider'll be in directly less'n he's in his cups. And Miss Isabele's expected soon. Just rest yourself. We're going to have a fine Southern dinner. Your folks from here?" she asked me.

"Mother's from Atlanta and my father was born in Beaufort, South Carolina."

"Mmmm-huh," she nodded, agreeing that these were certainly geographically fine folks.

"My people hail from Galway Bay," offered Neil.

"Well I'm sure they're mighty fine people too," she winked. "Now, is it for true," she whispered, setting the silverware, "you taking Mr. Ham to New York to sing?"

"We'd like to. But he doesn't seem very interested."

"Oh," she laughed, snapping the dishcloth across the table. "All that huffin' and puffin' don't signify. You know what he and Melanie been doing all day? Writing out the songs, the words. She's very smart, that girl. Make a fine secretary. I bet you could use a fine secretary with all that writing you do. There must be a lot of jobs . . ."

Neil saw it coming. He slouched in his seat and pushed his glasses up. He sat all the while rubbing his eyes. I fingered the soupspoon, vaguely attentive to Mama Teddy's monologue. It was perfectly clear what kind of game she was running. And why not? Along with the numerous tapes of chats and songfests, Neil had collected from the Delta and the Carolines a volume of tales that didn't go into the album catalogues, things he was saving for some sensational book he'd never write. The payoffs, bribes, bargains and deals, interviews in jail cells, drug wards, wino bins. Things apart from the usual folksy atrocity story. The romance had long since gone out of the job. Neil's first trauma occurred last spring when he finally smoked Bubba Mabley out of a corner. The sixty-year-old cardshark had insisted on taking his "little woman" along to New York. This sloe-eyed youngster of fifteen turned out to be his illegitimate daughter by his niece. It knocked Neil out, though he told it now with a certain rehearsed nonchalance.

"Mr. Rider wouldn't think of traveling without his family," the big woman was saying. "They're a very devoted family."

Neil had worked his eyes into a feverish red. But I was perfectly content. One good exploitive act deserved another. And what was the solitary old blues singer going to do after he had run the coffee-house circuit and scared the living shit out of the college kids? It was grotesque no matter how you cut it. I wished I was in films instead. Ole Ham Rider besieged by well-dressed coffee drinkers wanting his opinion on Miles Davis and Malcolm X was worth a few feet of film. And the quaint introduction some bearded fool in tight-across-the-groin pants would give would justify more footage. No amount of drunken thinking could convince me that Mr. Lyons could groom this character for popular hootenannies. On the other hand, if the militant civil liberties unions got hold of him, Mr. Charlie was a dead man.

"Here's Miss Isabele," the woman announced. She looked real enough to upset Lyons' plans. She shook hands and sat down, crossed her legs, and lit up a cigarette. She was good-looking in a way—plucked eyebrows, clinging wool dress, scary make-up. You knew she'd been jitterbugging since kindergarten, but she looked good anyhow.

"So you want the old man to sing," she said, sniffing in the curls of smoke. "Sits in the window sometimes to sing, but that don't cut no greens, don't make no coins." She swerved around in her chair and kicked Neil's foot. "The man needs money, mister. He's been needing for a long time. Now what you gonna do for him?"

"We're going to give him a chance to sing," Neil said,

catapulting a cigarette butt across the room with the table-
spoon.

She looked dissatisfied. "He needs," she said simply, send-
ing up a smoke screen. The image of the great old artist fallen
on bad times, holding up in a stuffy rooming house, drinking
bad home brew out of a jelly jar and howling blues out the
window appealed to my Grade-B movie-ruined mind. "Now,
when he gets here," Miss Isabele instructed me with her
cigarette, "you get him to do 'Evil Landlord.' That's his best."

"Will he bring his guitar?" Neil asked.

"He mostways do."

"To the dinner table?" Neil persisted.

"To the dinner table," she said, one eyebrow already on
its way to a threatening arch. "And I need a cigarette."

Mississippi Ham Rider brought his guitar and his granddaughter. He had on a white shirt and had left the greatcoat
at home. He mumbled his greetings and straddled a chair,
dislocating my leg in the process. "You got a long pair of legs,
sister."

I had no clever retort, so we all just sat there while Mama
Teddy heaved big bowls of things onto the table. There were
collard greens and black-eye peas and ham hocks and a long
pan of corn bread. And there were a whole lot of things I'd
never seen, even in my household.

"Bet you ain't ate like this in a long time," Rider said.
"Most people don't know how to cook nohow, 'specially you
Northerners."

"Jesus Christ," said Neil, leaning over to look into the
bowls on the far side of the table.

"What's that that smells?"

"That's the South, boy," said Rider. Melanie smiled and I
supposed the old man had made a joke. Neil leaned back and
got quiet. "I don't sing no cotton songs, sister," he said, picking up a knife. "And I ain't never worked in the fields or

shucked corn. And I don't sing no nappy-head church songs neither. And no sad numbers about losing my woman and losing my mind. I ain't never lost no woman and that's the truth." He sliced the corn bread with a ceremonial air.

"Good," I said for no particular reason. He looked up and for one rash moment I thought he was going to smile. I lost my head. But he really looked like he was going to work that bony, old, ashen skull in that direction.

"Well, what else is there?" Neil finally asked. "I mean just what kind of songs do you sing?"

"My kind."

Melanie smiled again and Miss Isabele laughed on her cigarette. But I was damned if I could get hold of this new kind of humor.

After we had eaten, Mama Teddy put coffee on the table and then tended to her customers. I stretched my legs into the aisle and relaxed, watching the old man work up his pipeful. He was impressive, the way a good demolition site can be, the way horror movies from the thirties are now. I was tempted to ask him how many people he had killed in his lifetime, thinking I had at last gotten hold of his vein of humor. But I sat and waited for him to sing. I was sure that on the first job he'd turn the place out and maybe do somebody in, just for the fun that was in it. And then a really weird thing came over me. I wanted to ask him a lot of dumb things about the South, about what he thought of the sit-ins and all. But he had already taken on a legendary air and was simply not of these times. I cursed Mr. Lyons' fairy-tale mentality and quietly indulged in fabricating figures from whole cloth.

"First I'm gonna sing you my birthday song," he said, pushing the coffee cups to the side. "And then I'm going to do this number about a little lady with long legs."

"Then what?" I smiled, putting my cup down.

"Then I'm gonna get drunk directly and pack my things. My bad suspenders and my green hat," he said. "One jar of

Noxzema and my stocking cap." Melanie laughed straight out and Neil began gagging on Miss Isabele's cigarette smoke. "And I gotta get a brand-new jug of Gallo," he sighed. "I don't never do no heavy traveling without my loving spoonful."

"Then you're coming with us?" I asked.

"We all going to New York and tear it up," he said.

"Damn," coughed Neil.

Rider grabbed his guitar by the neck and swung it over the dishes. He gave Neil a terrible look that only aggravated the coughing. "But first I think Mr. Somebody best go catch himself some air."

"I can take it," Neil growled, hooking up the tape recorder. He climbed over customers to get to the outlet. "It's on, man," he said. "Go ahead and sing your song." He looked up at Neil and then he did smile. I wouldn't ever want him to smile at me.

"I can take it," said Neil again, pushing up his glasses.

"See that you do, boy. See that you do." He plucked at the strings, grinning from ear to ear.

Happy
Birthday

OLLIE SPENT THE WHOLE MORNING WAITING. First she tried shaking Granddaddy Larkins, who just wouldn't wake up. She thought he was just playing, but he was out. His teeth weren't even in the glass, and there was a bottle on the bedstand. He'd be asleep for days. Then she waited on the cellar steps for Chalky, the building superintendent, to get through hauling garbage and come talk. But he was too busy. And then Ollie sat on the stairs waiting for Wilma. But it was Saturday and Wilma'd be holed up somewhere stuffing herself with potato chips and crunching down on jaw breakers, too greedy to cool it and eat 'em slow. Wilma'd come by tomorrow, though, and lie her behind off. "I went to Bear Mountain yesterday on a big boat with my brother Chestnut and his wife," she'd say, "and that's why I didn't come by for you cause we left so early in the morning that my mother even had to get me up when it was still dark out and we had a great time and I shot bows and arrows when we got there, and do you like my new dress?" Wilma always had some jive tale and always in one breath.

Ollie tried to figure out why she was even friends with Wilma. Wilma was going to grow up to be a lady and marry a doctor and live in New York, Wilma's mother said. But

Ollie, poor orphan, was going to grow up and marry a drinking man if she didn't get killed first, Wilma's mother said. Ollie never told Granddaddy Larkins what Wilma's mother was all the time saying. She just hated her in private.

Ollie spent the early afternoon sitting on the rail in front of The Chicken Shack Restaurant, watching the cooks sling the wire baskets of chicken in and out of the frying fat. They were too sweaty and tired to tell her to move from in front. "Ruining the business," the owner used to fuss. Later she stood between the laundry and shoe store, watching some men pitch pennies against the building. She waited for a while, squeezing a rubber ball in her hand. If I can just get the wall for a minute, she thought, maybe somebody'll come along and we'll have us a good game of handball. But the men went right on pitching while other ones were waiting their turn. They'd be there for hours, so Ollie left.

She knocked on Mrs. Robinson's door to see if she wanted her dog walked. It was cool in the hallway at least. No one was home, not even the loud-mouth dog that usually slammed itself against the door like he was big and bad instead of being just a sorry little mutt. Then Ollie took the stairs two at a time, swinging up past the fourth floor to the roof. There was rice all over. Ronnie must have already fed his pigeons. The door to the roof was unlocked, and that meant that the big boys were on the roof. She planted her behind against the door and pushed. She kicked at a cluster of rice. Some grains bounced onto the soft tar of the roof and sank. When Ollie moved onto the roof, the blinding sun made her squint. And there they were, the big boys, jammed between the skylight and the chimney like dummies in a window, just doing nothing and looking half-asleep.

Peter Proper, as always, was dressed to the teeth. "I naturally stays clean," he was always saying. Today he said nothing, just sitting. Marbles, a kid from the projects, had an open book on his knees. James was there, too, staring at a fingernail. And Ferman, the nut from crosstown, and Frenchie, the athlete. A flurry of cinders floated down from the chimney and settled into their hair like gray snow.

"Why don't you just sit in the incinerator? You can get even dirtier that way," Ollie yelled. No one moved or said anything. She expected Frenchie to at least say, "Here comes Miss Freshmouth," or for Peter to send her to the store for eighteen cents' worth of American cheese. It was always eighteen cents' worth, and he always handed her a quarter and a nickel. Big Time. "Don't none of you want nothing from the store today?" She squinted with her hands on her hips, waiting for the store dummies to start acting like Marbles, Peter, James, and so forth.

Ferman straightened out a leg against the skylight. "Ollie, when are you going to learn how to play with dolls?"

"Ya want anything from the store, Ferman Fruitcake? I'm too big for dolls." Ollie hitched up her jeans.

Ferman started to say something, but his audience was nearly asleep. Frenchie's head was nodding. James was staring into space. The pages of the open book on Marbles' knees were turning backward, three at a time, by themselves. Peter Proper was sitting very straight, back against the chimney with his eyes closed to the sun.

Ollie turned, looking over the edge of the roof. There was no one down in the park today. There was hardly anyone on the block. She propped a sticky foot against the roof railing and scraped off the tar. Everything below was gray as if the chimney had snowed on the whole block.

Chalky, the superintendent, was rolling a mattress onto a cart. Maybe he'd play cards with her. Just last Friday he had, but sometimes he wouldn't even remember her and would run and hide thinking she was King Kong come down just to hit him in the head or something. Ollie looked past the swings to the track. Empty. Frenchie should be out there trotting, she thought, looking back at him. He was dipping his head. Sometimes she'd trot beside Frenchie, taking big jumps to keep up. He'd smile at her but never teased her about them silly little jumps. He'd tell her for the hundredth time how he was going to enter the Olympics and walk off with a cup full of money.

"Go away, little girl!" Ferman had just yelled at her as if he had forgotten her name or didn't know her any more. He's as crazy as Chalky, thought Ollie, slamming the big roof door behind her and running down the stairs to the street. They must be brothers.

It was now four o'clock by the bank clock. Ollie remembered the bar-b-que place that had burned down. But she'd already rummaged through the ruins and found nothing. No use messing up her sneakers any further. She turned around to look the block over. Empty. Everyone was either at camp or at work or was sleeping like the boys on the roof or dead or just plain gone off. She perched on top of the fire hydrant with one foot, balancing with her arms. She could almost see into the high windows of Mount Zion A.M.E. Church. "This time I'm going to fly off and kill myself," she yelled, flapping her arms. A lady with bundles turned the corner and gave Ollie a look, crossed against the traffic, looking over her shoulder and shaking her head at what the kids of today had come to. Reverend Hall came out of the church basement, mopping his head with a big handkerchief.

"You go play somewhere else," he said, frowning into the sun.

"Where?" Ollie asked.

"Well, go to the park and play."

"With who?" she demanded. "I've got nobody to play with."

Reverend Hall just stood there trying to control his temper. He was always chasing the kids. That's why he's got no choir, Granddaddy Larkins was always saying. He always chases kids and dogs and pigeons and drunks.

"Little girl, you can't act up here in front of the church. Have you no—"

"How come you always calling me little girl, but you sure know my name when I'm walking with my grandfather?" Ollie said.

"Tell'm all about his sanctified self," said Miss Hazel, laughing out her window. But when the Reverend looked up to scowl, she ducked back in. He marched back into the church, shooing the pigeons off the steps.

"Wish me happy birthday," Ollie whispered to the pigeons. They hurried off toward the curb. "Better wish me happy birthday," she yelled, "or somebody around here is gonna get wasted."

Miss Hazel leaned out the window again. "What's with you, Ollie? You sick or something?"

"You should never have a birthday in the summertime," Ollie yelled, "cause nobody's around to wish you happy birthday or give you a party."

"Well, don't cry, sugar. When you get as old as me, you'll be glad to forget all about—"

"I'm not crying." Ollie stamped her foot, but the tears kept coming and before she could stop herself she was howling, right there in the middle of the street and not even caring who saw her. And she howled so loudly that even Miss Hazel's great-grandmother had to come to the window to see who was dying and with so much noise and on such a lovely day.

"What's the matter with the Larkins child?" asked the old woman.

"Beats me." Miss Hazel shook her head and watched Ollie for a minute. "I don't understand kids sometimes," she sighed, and closed the window so she could hear the television good.

Playin With Punjab

*F*IRST OF ALL, you don't play with Punjab. The man's got no sense of humor. On top of that, he's six-feet-something and solid hard. And not only that, he has an incredible memory and keeps unbelievably straight books. And he figures, I guess, that there ain't no sense of you dying from malnutrition when you can die so beautifully from a million and one other things and make the *Daily News* centerfold besides. So when Jackson from the projects put it this way: "Punjab, baby, I got this chick in a trick, and her mother's got my ass in a bind and I gots to live—" Punjab peeled three or four bills off the top with a dry finger (which is his way, dry) and told Jackson what the rates was. Now, you gotta figure Jackson for a dumb dude. All the sharks he could've snatched just by standing in front of the hamburger joint for a hot minute—higher rates maybe, but higher regard for your hide—and he goes to Punjab knowing damn well that he, Jackson, is a jive stud and a gameplayer and that he, Punjab, don't play with nobody. So like I said, this boy Jackson never did have his proper share of sense.

I'm sitting in the storefront with this gray lady, Miss Ruby, who came all the way out here to Brooklyn to straighten us folks out and get the rats taken care of and get us jobs and stuff like that, when here comes Jackson. Now this is several months later, and most of the block is sitting with Miss Ruby, helping her put her program on the street just by keeping the little kids off her car and bricks off her head and windows in her panes, and there comes Jackson. Everything's cool— the girl and all. But the day of reckoning is due, and like I say, Punjab don't play. Here comes Jackson in his Sunday suit with an arm swung around this Puerto Rican dude. What he's telling him is this: "Look, amigo my man, I got this boss place with furniture and windows and everything and a tub in the kitchen, so you don't even have to travel around for that morning bath. And the kitchen's painted the kind of yellow you'd dig on account of the super's one of you people. So for four beans you can move right in, and everything's yours. Don't have to mess with no boarding rooms and other shit. Send for your family in the morning. Square business."

Well, I said to Miss Ruby that I couldn't see the point of all that gumming and wearing out the teeth smiling and all. If the spic had four beans on him, walk him down toward the brewery and be done with it. But according to Newspaper (that's Gwen Southern, who's like the three monkeys reversed and inside out) Jackson didn't roll the guy. He set him up in the place just like he was saying. Need I say that the place went up in smoke that morning. And when Punjab got the word that Jackson had already split, he was bitter. Like I said, Jackson got in the wind. You'd get in the wind too if your ass was in hock to Punjab. We got the word that Jackson went into the army. For the third time, you understand. That's how untogether Jackson is: he needs to hide out that often that drastically. So if he knew anything at all about himself from the get-go, he never would've borrowed. And if he didn't know anything about his ownself, he should've asked somebody. So he went into the army. Didn't do no good. Got iced the same day he got out. And Jackson's mother wound up hocking damn near everything she had ever bought on time or no. But that's another story.

The story I wants to tell is about the block, I guess, and about how Miss Ruby found out that Punjab don't play. I say Miss Ruby because I myself already knew, cause my mother knew a whole lotta Punjabs in her day and passed this onto me along with the vitamins and the dextrose and all them other nutrients that comes tubing in when you're huddled up there in the dark waiting to get born. It was hopping time. And when it's hopping time in Brooklyn, I usually hauls my ashes over to one of them centers where there's a lot of scary workers with an open line to the cops. Any other time I'm all for working with the realer type people who get right out there in the street with all the jitterbugs and take your side against the landlords and the cops. That's fine for wintertime when there ain't so much wine-drinking and stoop-sitting and head-whipping. But in summer that can be dangerous, the streets. So after the Field Day tryouts I put it to Miss Ruby like this: "Look here, Miss Ruby, I gots to get my typing up and get one of them jobs in the center around the way cause summer's coming on and the block's going to be holy hell."

She looked me dead in the eye and said: "I need you right here with me to translate, Violet, cause you know I don't speak negro too tough." I thought that was pretty cute, but I went right ahead with my typing practice, reading the dictionary, and getting my suit together for one of them interviews they always put you through even if you're only asking to swing the stupid stick and wash windows.

But it turned out to be a cool summer. Hot in all the usual ways, but no jitterbugging. Even in the air-conditioned diner where we ate at, everything was hot and muggy. You could smell sour milk and mushy watermelon all day long. Your coffee was always full of cinders, and everybody looked grim and grimy, and all the dogs looked like they had rabies or something. And one of the piers caught on fire for no reason I know of except everything was burning up including me. But everything was law and orderly. Even the little kids were straight and legal about not opening up the johnny pumps. The only people up to their old tricks was Punjab and Punjab's grandfather, who sat on the trash can giving advice on single action.

How she worked it I'm not sure. I can guess, but ain't no use telling everything I know. I've seen her do some unbelievable things with landlords and with cops and with truant officers and storekeepers with weird scales, even with the old West Indian lady, Miss Bunch, who never let anybody get into her place, not even the meter reader, much less some fay chick. Well, I actually saw Miss Ruby lead that lady out of 575 into the light of day, over to the center to speak into the tape recorder, down to the church basement to pick up on the senior citizens club, and back. But how she actually worked her thing on Punjab is anybody's guess unless you happen to have some theories about men, about Black men particularly, and especially about Southern Black men and their thing about white women. My theory is the Black man got jammed up by the White man's nightmare. But anyway, it must've been Punjab what called cool cause there ain't nobody else big enough on the block to do it.

She opened his nose is how she did it. Like I'd be at the phone, contacting all these lames she was trying to set a fire under so they'd build a clinic and be civil to the junkies round our way, and here comes Punjab. Not with the flashy car and his even flashier henchmen, but walking up the block alone like any normal, everyday-type person. And he's peeping through the window grinning up a storm. Not like him at all who can be viewed at any hour of day or night slapping some chick upside the head or collecting coins from this barfly or that. And let Miss Ruby ask him to do something. Like a

72

centipede stumbling fast over every single one of them legs. Or I'm cranking the mimeo cause she was a bug about keeping the block informed as to the latest thing we was getting swindled out of because we wouldn't organize, and here he comes again with beer or cigarettes or something. I'll say this for Punjab: I've seen a whole lot of piercing scenes go down in his name, but he was never close with the money. Like the time he brung this great pot of ribs and potato salad, followed up by a pan of hopping john and a gallon of Gallo. Embarrassing, cause I was off the clock already and had no real reason to hang around except that I likes to grit and am partial to that loving spoonful. I grit back, I won't lie.

What happened was this, to make a long story short. Not only had he called cool, but he'd also put up bail a couple of times for some of the star pupils Miss Ruby called herself rehabilitating. One of these stars split, but Punjab didn't go after him. Not only that, Punjab had also stomped a few heads by the subway garage on account of them staring too hard at Miss Ruby's hips and saying things. All in all, Miss Ruby was making puppy tracks in Punjab's books. So that fall when she was knocking everybody out to set up an election to pick community leaders to represent us on the poverty council and all over the place, we figured Punjab for a natural. We figured he was going to get paid off finally. Hell, let's face it, anybody in position to be calling themself doing good is always doing well, if you know what I mean. And there was a whole lotta long bread coming into our area. So we figured Punjab was going to get his cut, him being the only kind of leader we could even think of. Matter of fact, most people didn't even bother to come down and cram that yellow card into the milk box. But at the rally, she actually counted all those cards and came up with this cornball preacher who used to double as Santa Claus during the holidays, and Ann Silver's grandmother, stone nose. These were our delegates. Needless to say, we acted up. Then Miss Ruby got warm. First time I ever heard her curse.

"If you didn't exercise your right as a voter, shut the hell up. That's what the cards say. That's it."

Miss Elaine from 579 got up, patting her throat and fleshy bosom and came right out with what everybody was sitting there sweating and thinking. "Now you knows as well as I, Miss Ruby darling, that Mr. Punjab should be one of them peoples what go to places and talk with the Man. So I don't even see no sense whatever to these cards."

"Well, why didn't you all vote for Mr. Punjab?" Miss Ruby's hair was getting wild.

Then sister Taylor got up to say that she wasn't for Rebum Smothers representing her block since he was so busy aping the white churches that he had lost his gospel choir. "And not only that," she said, jabbing a finger in the air, "he don't talk good enough to be no delegate. Cain't nobody hardly understand him lessen you came from wherever he be from." She also had a few things to say to Miss Ruby about all this "grass roots" and "poor folks" and other phrases she didn't like coming out of no white mouth, but everybody kept signaling her and whispering and whatnot till she finally reached back and pulled her dress away from her sticky thighs. Didn't do no good. Soon as she got started again the dress would ride up, and she was too embarrassed to put her hand where it needed to get to pull that dress straight, so she sat down.

"Reverend Smothers and Mrs. Silver are our representatives," said Miss Ruby. "All block captains will meet with them to discuss what you feel should be said in the way of demands at the meeting. Adjourned."

I wasn't around when Punjab came to collect, so to speak. All I can tell you is what Newspaper ran down to me; and I can, of course, describe to you how the office looked. But, then, anybody could've bust in and messed up the place. Me and some of the other girls hung around there for days waiting for Miss Ruby to show up. Only person what came was some guy in an official-looking gray car with a clipboard. He asked some questions and wrote on this clipboard. But you know how dumb Black people can be when they want to. But Sneaker shot off his mouth about how he should've been paid for all his leg work regardless of Punjab's debt. He went on to say that Miss Ruby was full of shit with all her foolishness about power and equality and responsibility and sacrifice, and then cop right out when the chips were down. He said a few choice things more about ass standin in the way of progress, but then Sneaker always did have a crude-type mouth. The cat in the gray car went on about his business, and we went on about ours. And that was that.

"Come on and walk me," Sneaker was saying, pulling on my girl friend. "Gots to go see Punjab about a job. Least he don't play around with your money."

We walked Sneaker up to the poolroom to wait for Punjab to come around that corner on two white walls. He always did on the third and the eighteenth.

Talking
Bout
Sonny

"SOMETHING CAME OVER ME." That was all we could report when we got back to the block. That was all we heard. Very likely all he had said.

"Hell of a thing to say," said Lee, shaking his head.

"Well, what you supposed to say when you just got through putting a knife in your wife's neck? After a gesture like that you want eloquence too?"

"Well, I don't understand it myself," said Lee. "Just to stand there with blood all over your shirt, stand there and look the Man in the face and say that something came over you, like that was some kind of explanation."

"Oh, man, you irritate my ass," said Delauney, screwing up his face. "The cat's just another angry dude that iced his wife. A Southern orator you want. You stand there in that damn fool apron making all kind of off-the-wall demands on the guy and—" Delauney turned to me. "You understand it, don't you, baby? I mean 'Something came over me' comes through to you, don't it?" I nodded and he swung around to the bartender again. "You see. You're the only insensitive and stupid bastard around here. Nothing up here," he tapped his head. "Didn't nothing ever come over you? No, I guess not. You too damned dead, that's what. A bottle-tipping vegetable mother."

Lee didn't say anything. He wiped his hands slowly across the apron doubled over his belly. And then, very deliberately, he gave me a refill on the house as if to say he knew what I had on my hands. Or maybe he just dug where Delauney was at and was sympathetic, knowing he had to scream on someone. And what better mark than a big, fat, sloppy bartender that never did anybody any harm?

"Now, what happens to me sometimes is like that." He swiveled around to me again. "I can wake up, not thinking anything in particular, and all of a sudden it's on me. A cloud of evil. A fit of nastiness takes over. Next thing you know I'm doing dirty to everybody and giving out with the malevolent looks, as you know I can. Like sometimes, I just hate all people, that's all. And I pass 'em in the streets and cut 'em dead. Or I can spy that fire axe in the glass cage and get to thinking how I'd just love to take the thing to work with me and really work out. And maybe this thing'll go on all day. So you figure that for some people these dark days just kind of build up and then that . . . that . . ." He stopped, searching for the definitive gesture. "That cloud of evil like zooms in on you . . . like a capsule moment, you dig? Fifty-some-odd days of pure shit jammed into one mad moment and boom —you plant a razor in your wife's throat." He nodded to himself in the bar mirror, satisfied that he had got the thing out and wishing, I guess, that he could've been telling it to someone who mattered, who could make a difference in his friend's fate now. "Yeah," he nodded again, picking up his drink, "that's how it must've been with Sonny. One of them things."

I don't know about this particular thing that came over Sonny last Saturday afternoon, when the rest of the guys were out in the park hustling and I was sweating away in the kitchen like a damn fool, knowing Delauney has never been on time for Sunday dinner anyhow, but I'd seen a thing or two come on Sonny before. Like the day the girls led me by the hand to meet their daddy. And there they all were, Buddy from the projects who grew up with me; Teddy who used to hang out with my brother's crowd; a tall, bowlegged stud named Richie the Goof; and the leader of the group, the girl's father (who turned out to be Delauney); and, of course, Sonny. Sonny was charging down the court and everybody on the side was chanting, "Drive, Sonny, drive." And all of a sudden—nobody near him to block or fluster, all alone with his eyes riveted on the rim and his wrist about to stop that ball loose and send it gliding up towards the tips of the fingers for that last sure push—all of a sudden he just froze and his face tightened up like the skin had become bones, and this tremor came up out of his socks and caterpillared up the calves to the thighs. You could see the shivering in the ass before it wriggled up then down the spine. Just then, everybody came down the court, just becoming aware that something was up and very much the matter.

"Shoot, baby, shoot." And staring in disbelief and puzzlement and a little disgust and impatience too. And then Sonny just doubled over on top of the ball, clutching it to him. They had to carry him and the ball off the court in tandem, like a piece of sculpture. (The girls thought he was playing 'statues' like we do at the center.)

"Oh hell, ain't nothing wrong with Sonny," said Delauney that Monday when he invited me over for breakfast with him and the girls. "He's just getting a little too old for park ball, that's all."

"But aren't you worried?" I persisted late into the afternoon. "I mean if he has these fits all the time—"

"Not all the time . . . look, forget about it. I'm sure he has already."

"Well, he really ought to see a doctor about those seizures."

81

"Seizures?" Delauney tilted back his chair to laugh. "Leave it to a chick to blow a nothing into a big deal. Ain't no big deal. Sonny's just tired. Your muscles buckle on you like that sometimes. He'll get over it; he always does. Ain't no sense making a big thing about it."

Beverly was stretched out on the couch waiting for Delauney to fix her skates. I just sat, listening to some spiritual station that was slipping off into static. Delauney just sat there, too, biting on his mustache and moving his coffee cup around in the saucer like he was thinking it over. Beverly was doing her best to wait patiently, fidgeting just a little, cracking the plastic slipcovers that kept sticking to her damp legs.

It was probably my concern for Beverly and Arlene more than for Sonny that made me wonder about Delauney's unconcern. Suppose fever was no big deal either, or a bad cough, or mysterious spots in the mouth just nothing? Arlene came and sat in my lap, also waiting for her father to make a move. Absent-mindedly, she began poking her fingers through the holes in the oilcloth tablecloth. Next thing I knew, I was digging a finger into the holes in the upholstered chair, the raggedy touch of the plastic and the wooly insides sort of soothing me out of worry that was not mine anyway. They weren't my kids, for crying out loud. He wasn't my father. And I wasn't Florence Nightingale. And maybe, I thought, maybe Delauney's shrugging-off attitude only applies to his basketball buddies. What the hell, I'm sure he's a good father.

"What are you doing, monkeyface?" he said suddenly, slapping Arlene's hand away from the oilskin. "Why don't you two go on out and play so me and Miss Butler can talk."

"You were going to fix the skates, Daddy." He chewed on his mustache some more, then got up. I guess I got to be a drag about it, not because I'd taken a sudden interest in neurology, Sonny's nervous system in particular, but because I was very fond of the girls. And I really wasn't up to any fantasizing—I in white robes and with bleeding heart rescue the innocents from the step-ugly ogre. Occupational hazard of social workers. I needed to be convinced that Delauney was neither an ogre or a disinterested person. I guess I got sickening about it.

"Oh hell, Betty, let's not start that up again. Look, Sonny's a grown man and you're not his mother. Matter of fact, you ain't nobody's mother, and I wish to hell you'd cut out this nursery-school-marm shit. Man," he told the window pane, "women get on my ass. Truly."

"Is that why you spend so much time with the boys? Boys, my foot. I wish you could see yourselves, big overgrown dudes running around in sneakers hustling kids for nickels and dimes. It's sickening. Delauney, when are you going to grow up?"

"Now, look," finger in my face and eyes slit, "the last chick that started in with that shit get her behind put out on the sidewalk with nothing but a handful of change to get her home to mother. And that was my wife. And if I don't take that crap from my own wife, you know I ain't going to put—"

"You don't have to. This is my apartment, remember?"

"Okay. Okay," he said and went back to chewing on his mustache. I was almost sorry I'd pressed him into it. But just that morning they had come by and picked me up to go to Brooklyn, fresh territory, to watch them operate. They lost three out of five. Sonny said I was a jinx and proceeded to pick his sneakers apart. First, off came the bicycle patches; then out came the laces. He ripped the sneakers to shreds. Just stood there very quietly by the car while we were all drinking beer, stood there and ripped open the sneakers and tore them apart. No one batted an eye.

"Well, maybe his lawyer will plead insanity," offered Lee, wiping off the bar and emptying Delauney's ashtray. "Damn shame. Nice guy."

Delauney dropped his head into his hands and waited for Lee to move up the counter. "Don't that just grab you, people who say dumb things like that? What does he know? Maybe she had it coming. Maybe that was the most beautiful thing Sonny has ever done in his whole life, killing the bitch—"

"Delauney, she was real nice. You liked her."

"You never know. Nice. Who's to say? The point is . . ." His gesture remained incomplete as well. And spotting himself in the blue of the mirror, he got too self-conscious about the waving arms to pick up the thread. "The point is . . ." He played with a book of matches, eyeing me suspiciously as if I were somehow to blame for the whole thing. "I suppose you're going to pull one of those I-told-you-so things on me real soon. Huh, Betty? And then sit there self-righteously accusing me of . . ." He lost that thread, too.

"Well, Delauney," I said, "there's nothing we can do about anything now."

"Yeah, well . . . hell, ain't his fault. Poor bastard."

"What do you mean it's not his fault?"

"Look, stupid, it is nobody's fault—nobody's. Something just came over him, that's all. These things happen. Right?" He grabbed hold of Lee's apron as he passed. "You've had that happen to you, huh Lee? Something just take hold of you and you're not yourself. You're not anyone or . . . anything, not responsible for yourself or what you do, or for anybody else. That's how it must've been."

"Yeah, I guess so," said Lee, looking at me and waiting for me to tip my empty glass his way.

The
Lesson

*B*ACK IN THE DAYS when everyone was old and stupid or young and foolish and me and Sugar were the only ones just right, this lady moved on our block with nappy hair and proper speech and no makeup. And quite naturally we laughed at her, laughed the way we did at the junk man who went about his business like he was some big-time president and his sorry-ass horse his secretary. And we kinda hated her too, hated the way we did the winos who cluttered up our parks and pissed on our handball walls and stank up our hallways and stairs so you couldn't halfway play hide-and-seek without a goddamn gas mask. Miss Moore was her name. The only woman on the block with no first name. And she was black as hell, cept for her feet, which were fish-white and spooky. And she was always planning these boring-ass things for us to do, us being my cousin, mostly, who lived on the block cause we all moved North the same time and to the same apartment then spread out gradual to breathe. And our parents would yank our heads into some kinda shape and crisp up our clothes so we'd be presentable for travel with Miss Moore, who always looked like she was going to church, though she never did. Which is just one of things the grown-ups talked about when they talked behind her back like a

dog. But when she came calling with some sachet she'd
sewed up or some gingerbread she'd made or some book,
why then they'd all be too embarrassed to turn her down and
we'd get handed over all spruced up. She'd been to college
and said it was only right that she should take responsibility
for the young ones' education, and she not even related by
marriage or blood. So they'd go for it. Specially Aunt
Gretchen. She was the main gofer in the family. You got
some ole dumb shit foolishness you want somebody to go for,
you send for Aunt Gretchen. She been screwed into the
go-along for so long, it's a blood-deep natural thing with her.
Which is how she got saddled with me and Sugar and Junior
in the first place while our mothers were in a la-de-da apartment up the block having a good ole time.

So this one day Miss Moore rounds us all up at the mailbox
and it's puredee hot and she's knockin herself out about
arithmetic. And school suppose to let up in summer I heard,
but she don't never let up. And the starch in my pinafore
scratching the shit outta me and I'm really hating this nappy-
head bitch and her goddamn college degree. I'd much rather
go to the pool or to the show where it's cool. So me and Sugar
leaning on the mailbox being surly, which is a Miss Moore
word. And Flyboy checking out what everybody brought for
lunch. And Fat Butt already wasting his peanut-butter-and-
jelly sandwich like the pig he is. And Junebug punchin on
Q.T.'s arm for potato chips. And Rosie Giraffe shifting from
one hip to the other waiting for somebody to step on her foot
or ask her if she from Georgia so she can kick ass, preferably
Mercedes'. And Miss Moore asking us do we know what
money is, like we a bunch of retards. I mean real money, she
say, like it's only poker chips or monopoly papers we lay on
the grocer. So right away I'm tired of this and say so. And
would much rather snatch Sugar and go to the Sunset and
terrorize the West Indian kids and take their hair ribbons
and their money too. And Miss Moore files that remark away

for next week's lesson on brotherhood, I can tell. And finally I say we oughta get to the subway cause it's cooler and besides we might meet some cute boys. Sugar done swiped her mama's lipstick, so we ready.

So we heading down the street and she's boring us silly about what things cost and what our parents make and how much goes for rent and how money ain't divided up right in this country. And then she gets to the part about we all poor and live in the slums, which I don't feature. And I'm ready to speak on that, but she steps out in the street and hails two cabs just like that. Then she hustles half the crew in with her and hands me a five-dollar bill and tells me to calculate 10 percent tip for the driver. And we're off. Me and Sugar and Junebug and Flyboy hangin out the window and hollering to everybody, putting lipstick on each other cause Flyboy a faggot anyway, and making farts with our sweaty armpits. But I'm mostly trying to figure how to spend this money. But they all fascinated with the meter ticking and Junebug starts laying bets as to how much it'll read when Flyboy can't hold his breath no more. Then Sugar lays bets as to how much it'll be when we get there. So I'm stuck. Don't nobody want to go for my plan, which is to jump out at the next light and run off to the first bar-b-que we can find. Then the driver tells us to get the hell out cause we there already. And the meter reads eighty-five cents. And I'm stalling to figure out the tip and Sugar say give him a dime. And I decide he don't need it bad as I do, so later for him. But then he tries to take off with Junebug foot still in the door so we talk about his mama something ferocious. Then we check out that we on Fifth Avenue and everybody dressed up in stockings. One lady in a fur coat, hot as it is. White folks crazy.

"This is the place," Miss Moore say, presenting it to us in the voice she uses at the museum. "Let's look in the windows before we go in."

"Can we steal?" Sugar asks very serious like she's getting

the ground rules squared away before she plays. "I beg your pardon," say Miss Moore, and we fall out. So she leads us around the windows of the toy store and me and Sugar screamin, "This is mine, that's mine, I gotta have that, that was made for me, I was born for that," till Big Butt drowns us out.

"Hey, I'm goin to buy that there."

"That there? You don't even know what it is, stupid."

"I do so," he say punchin on Rosie Giraffe. "It's a microscope."

"Whatcha gonna do with a microscope, fool?"

"Look at things."

"Like what, Ronald?" ask Miss Moore. And Big Butt ain't got the first notion. So here go Miss Moore gabbing about the thousands of bacteria in a drop of water and the somethinorother in a speck of blood and the million and one living things in the air around us is invisible to the naked eye. And what she say that for? Junebug go to town on that "naked" and we rolling. Then Miss Moore ask what it cost. So we all jam into the window smudgin it up and the price tag say $300. So then she ask how long'd take for Big Butt and Junebug to save up their allowances. "Too long," I say. "Yeh," adds Sugar, "outgrown it by that time." And Miss Moore say no, you never outgrow learning instruments. "Why, even medical students and interns and," blah, blah, blah. And we ready to choke Big Butt for bringing it up in the first damn place.

"This here costs four hundred eighty dollars," say Rosie Giraffe. So we pile up all over her to see what she pointin out. My eyes tell me it's a chunk of glass cracked with something heavy, and different-color inks dripped into the splits, then the whole thing put into a oven or something. But for $480 it don't make sense.

"That's a paperweight made of semi-precious stones fused together under tremendous pressure," she explains slowly, with her hands doing the mining and all the factory work.

"So what's a paperweight?" asks Rosie Giraffe.

"To weigh paper with, dumbbell," say Flyboy, the wise man from the East.

"Not exactly," say Miss Moore, which is what she say when you warm or way off too. "It's to weigh paper down so it won't scatter and make your desk untidy." So right away me and Sugar curtsy to each other and then to Mercedes who is more the tidy type.

"We don't keep paper on top of the desk in my class," say Junebug, figuring Miss Moore crazy or lyin one.

"At home, then," she say. "Don't you have a calendar and a pencil case and a blotter and a letter-opener on your desk at home where you do your homework?" And she know damn well what our homes look like cause she nosys around in them every chance she gets.

"I don't even have a desk," say Junebug. "Do we?"

"No. And I don't get no homework neither," say Big Butt.

"And I don't even have a home," say Flyboy like he do at school to keep the white folks off his back and sorry for him. Send this poor kid to camp posters, is his specialty.

"I do," says Mercedes. "I have a box of stationery on my desk and a picture of my cat. My godmother bought the stationery and the desk. There's a big rose on each sheet and the envelopes smell like roses."

"Who wants to know about your smelly-ass stationery," say Rosie Giraffe fore I can get my two cents in.

"It's important to have a work area all your own so that . . ."

"Will you look at this sailboat, please," say Flyboy, cuttin her off and pointin to the thing like it was his. So once again we tumble all over each other to gaze at this magnificent thing in the toy store which is just big enough to maybe sail two kittens across the pond if you strap them to the posts tight. We all start reciting the price tag like we in assembly. "Handcrafted sailboat of fiberglass at one thousand one hundred ninety-five dollars."

"Unbelievable," I hear myself say and am really stunned. I read it again for myself just in case the group recitation put me in a trance. Same thing. For some reason this pisses me off. We look at Miss Moore and she lookin at us, waiting for I dunno what.

"Who'd pay all that when you can buy a sailboat set for a quarter at Pop's, a tube of glue for a dime, and a ball of string for eight cents? "It must have a motor and a whole lot else besides," I say. "My sailboat cost me about fifty cents."

"But will it take water?" say Mercedes with her smart ass.

"Took mine to Alley Pond Park once," say Flyboy. "String broke, Lost it. Pity."

"Sailed mine in Central Park and it keeled over and sank. Had to ask my father for another dollar."

"And you got the strap," laugh Big Butt. "The jerk didn't even have a string on it. My old man wailed on his behind."

Little Q.T. was staring hard at the sailboat and you could see he wanted it bad. But he too little and somebody'd just take it from him. So what the hell. "This boat for kids, Miss Moore?"

"Parents silly to buy something like that just to get all broke up," say Rosie Giraffe.

"That much money it should last forever," I figure.

"My father'd buy it for me if I wanted it."

"Your father, my ass," say Rosie Giraffe getting a chance to finally push Mercedes.

"Must be rich people shop here," say Q.T.

"You are a very bright boy," say Flyboy. "What was your first clue?" And he rap him on the head with the back of his knuckles, since Q.T. the only one he could get away with. Though Q.T. liable to come up behind you years later and get his licks in when you half expect it.

"What I want to know is," I says to Miss Moore though I never talk to her, I wouldn't give the bitch that satisfaction, "is how much a real boat costs? I figure a thousand'd get you a yacht any day."

"Why don't you check that out," she says, "and report back to the group?" Which really pains my ass. If you gonna mess up a perfectly good swim day least you could do is have some answers. "Let's go in," she say like she got something up her sleeve. Only she don't lead the way. So me and Sugar turn the corner to where the entrance is, but when we get there I kinda hang back. Not that I'm scared, what's there to be afraid of, just a toy store. But I feel funny, shame. But what I got to be shamed about? Got as much right to go in as anybody. But somehow I can't seem to get hold of the door, so I step away for Sugar to lead. But she hangs back too. And I look at her and she looks at me and this is ridiculous. I mean, damn, I have never ever been shy about doing nothing or going nowhere. But then Mercedes steps up and then Rosie Giraffe and Big Butt crowd in behind and shove, and next thing we all stuffed into the doorway with only Mercedes squeezing past us, smoothing out her jumper and walking right down the aisle. Then the rest of us tumble in like a glued-together jigsaw done all wrong. And people lookin at us. And it's like the time me and Sugar crashed into the Catholic church on a dare. But once we got in there and everything so hushed and holy and the candles and the bow-in and the handkerchiefs on all the drooping heads, I just couldn't go through with the plan. Which was for me to run up to the altar and do a tap dance while Sugar played the nose flute and messed around in the holy water. And Sugar kept givin me the elbow. Then later teased me so bad I tied her up in the shower and turned it on and locked her in. And she'd be there till this day if Aunt Gretchen hadn't finally figured I was lyin about the boarder takin a shower.

Same thing in the store. We all walkin on tiptoe and

hardly touchin the games and puzzles and things. And I watched Miss Moore who is steady watchin us like she waitin for a sign. Like Mama Drewery watches the sky and sniffs the air and takes note of just how much slant is in the bird formation. Then me and Sugar bump smack into each other, so busy gazing at the toys, 'specially the sailboat. But we don't laugh and go into our fat-lady bump-stomach routine. We just stare at that price tag. Then Sugar run a finger over the whole boat. And I'm jealous and want to hit her. Maybe not her, but I sure want to punch somebody in the mouth.

"Watcha bring us here for, Miss Moore?"

"You sound angry, Sylvia. Are you mad about something?" Givin me one of them grins like she tellin a grown-up joke that never turns out to be funny. And she's lookin very closely at me like maybe she plannin to do my portrait from memory. I'm mad, but I won't give her that satisfaction. So I slouch around the store bein very bored and say, "Let's go."

Me and Sugar at the back of the train watchin the tracks whizzin by large then small then gettin gobbled up in the dark. I'm thinkin about this tricky toy I saw in the store. A clown that somersaults on a bar then does chin-ups just cause you yank lightly at his leg. Cost $35. I could see me askin my mother for a $35 birthday clown. "You wanna who that costs what?" she'd say, cocking her head to the side to get a better view of the hole in my head. Thirty-five dollars could buy new bunk beds for Junior and Gretchen's boy. Thirty-five dollars and the whole household could go visit Granddaddy Nelson in the country. Thirty-five dollars would pay for the rent and the piano bill too. Who are these people that spend that much for performing clowns and $1,000 for toy sailboats? What kinda work they do and how they live and how come we ain't in on it? Where we are is who we are, Miss Moore always pointin out. But it don't necessarily have to be that way, she always adds then waits for somebody to say that poor people have to wake up and demand their share of the pie and don't none of us know what kind of pie she talkin about in the first damn place. But she ain't so smart cause I still got her four dollars from the taxi and she sure ain't gettin it. Messin up my day with this shit. Sugar nudges me in my pocket and winks.

Miss Moore lines us up in front of the mailbox where we started from, seem like years ago, and I got a headache for thinkin so hard. And we lean all over each other so we can hold up under the draggy-ass lecture she always finishes us off with at the end before we thank her for borin us to tears. But she just looks at us like she readin tea leaves. Finally she say, "Well, what did you think of F.A.O. Schwartz?"

Rosie Giraffe mumbles, "White folks crazy."

"I'd like to go there again when I get my birthday money," says Mercedes, and we shove her out the pack so she has to lean on the mailbox by herself.

"I'd like a shower. Tiring day," say Flyboy.

Then Sugar surprises me by sayin, "You know, Miss Moore, I don't think all of us here put together eat in a year what that sailboat costs." And Miss Moore lights up like somebody goosed her. "And?" she say, urging Sugar on. Only I'm standin on her foot so she don't continue.

"Imagine for a minute what kind of society it is in which some people can spend on a toy what it would cost to feed a family of six or seven. What do you think?"

"I think," say Sugar pushing me off her feet like she never done before, cause I whip her ass in a minute, "that this is not much of a democracy if you ask me. Equal chance to pursue happiness means an equal crack at the dough, don't it?" Miss Moore is besides herself and I am disgusted with Sugar's treachery. So I stand on her foot one more time to see if she'll shove me. She shuts up, and Miss Moore looks at me, sorrowfully I'm thinkin. And somethin weird is goin on, I can feel it in my chest.

"Anybody else learn anything today?" lookin dead at me.

95

I walk away and Sugar has to run to catch up and don't even seem to notice when I shrug her arm off my shoulder.

"Well, we got four dollars anyway," she says.

"Uh hunh."

"We could go to Hascombs and get half a chocolate layer and then go to the Sunset and still have plenty money for potato chips and ice-cream sodas."

"Uh hunh."

"Race you to Hascombs," she say.

We start down the block and she gets ahead which is O.K. by me cause I'm goin to the West End and then over to the Drive to think this day through. She can run if she want to and even run faster. But ain't nobody gonna beat me at nuthin.

The
Survivor

JEWEL AWOKE half expecting to find herself in the recovery room, overwhelmed with sorrow and weeping over an irretrievable loss, till she remembered it was only her tonsils after all, and the sobbing was more a result of the Sodium Pentothal than her state of mind. But that was years ago. Today she was waking up on a speeding bus, and a bus ride is a dangerous thing. The mind off guard, an easy mark for all the one-part dreams three-fourths forgot that sprocket themselves and urge the cameras to run amok. Brother Billy on a dare leaping blindfold from a cliff in Morningside Park. The aged super, her friend over the checkerboard, being removed from the cellar on a dingy stretcher, starved to death, left to wait on the curb while the attendants grabbed a smoke and she shrieked, impotent. Carl Berry, who early, tenderly, gave her to herself, walking off the roof—the final high. Greatgranddaddy Spencer with emptied eyes strapped down under the rubber sheets as they turned him on like Frankenstein and she had signed and he had begged but she had signed . . .

Her feet in the stirrups, drifting away from herself, but another her in attendance as the coal miner with the cyclops eye dumped hunks of her, the best of her, ruby quartz and reeking, down the drain, as if digging out a diseased portion of a dangerous vein, and for so long she felt herself coming back to herself to meet the pain too soon—snipping my wings, no, freeing me from disease—so long as if very huge portions were malign—seems so much of me is malign—then drifting somewhere else where it was flannel-warm and quiet. But that was years ago.

the vans coming in the night to haul away everything in liquor boxes marked "this side up" when everything else was upside down now that the man with the rolled-up sleeves was the man conducting the orchestra of cameras was the man bent over the editing bin was the man leaning over her breasts and rolling away to become just a very dead mister

Wives, she'd learned growing up in the dark, were the ladies found tied to scuttled boats at the bottom of the lake, their hair embraced by the seaweed. Husbands were men with their heads bashed in, doused with alcohol, stuck under the driver's wheel, and shoved over the cliff. Wives were tautly strung creatures you plotted against with optical illusions, tape recorders, coincidences, and evil servants until they went mad and you inherited the estate. Husbands were dull sofas you schemed against with your convertible boyfriends who knew how to talk him into increasing his insurance at the critical moment. Wives were victims pushed beyond endurance, then snatched suddenly back from the edge by that final straw we carry from birth just in time to butcher beer bellies in the bedroom. Husbands were worms that turned on the *femmes fatales* who were too cocky to plot his death and got strangled with piano wire

Jewel had once, after one of their fiercer arguments, taken a safety pin and stuck him stark dead. And when he came from the bathroom, half-shaven and suspicious at the sudden lull in the war, saw his impaled photograph and broke the cap off her two front teeth.

"They're predicting six inches of snow by nightfall and gale winds besides," said the man next to her. He tapped the window and flakes of snow shifted patterns then slid off the glass like rain. Jewel glanced unconcerned at the landscape rushing by. The trees looked as if something unnatural had been done to them.

"Mmm," she replied, and smoothed the book out again on what little lap left in the ninth month. But before she could recall what she was reading, her eyes slipped off the edge of the glossy page to drown in the shadows of her hip, then buoy up again and swivel onto the back of the worn seat in front of her, fastening onto a clump of frayed threads beckoning, accusing, with each bump of the bus. She shifted her weight, not so much to balance the baby, as to juggle the mind's dangers, to ease the shouting in the head less it become a banging on the wall—let me go mad, Grandmother. Let me bleed and be forever lost and no one. The bus rushing through the whitened country to the old woman who could dispel the incubus devouring her with a simple laying on of the hands.

"Hope we make it to town before it starts gusting," said the man, offering a stick of gum. Jewel slid her eyes deep back in their sockets and played dead.

he had stumbled in with his throat slit, grabbed his neck with all ten fingers as if to plug up the dike. The blood so bright, that's what paralyzed her as he gurgled to take command, one hand on top of the other and shoulders hunched as if to keep his head from falling off. And she fainting there, registering only briefly the seismographic shocks in her blood, then failing to register anything at all. She had come to to find them attending him on the kitchen table, the

*fluorescent light from the sink yanked out and strung up
over the window shutters, the wires trailing over his body,
the light casting a green blue on the rusty suture banding his
neck. And he had lived. Never to organize again or turn his
cameras on anything but actors, on mostly her. And nothing
was ever said about he could've died. She fainting killing
him. Nothing said but not forgotten, in his bloodstream
keeping him from coming to her with her, keeping him from
her. And coiled in her memory, springing at the last, seizing
her at the casket and spinning her right around to hurl her
into the collapsible chairs and up under the flowers, smother-
ing.*

"Be there in ten minutes, the driver said," the man announced, smiling at the bulge in her lap. "I know you'll be
glad to get comfortable. When my wife was pregnant, and
she's tall with long legs like you . . ."

Ten minutes. No bearings. Her past scattered about her
and the mind all cluttered, no room to think in. Ten minutes.
Grandmother Candy will want to talk. Jewel cleared her
throat, fearing she had lost all words. Frantic, she assembled
a simple sentence of greeting and announcement of exhaus-
tion. That would be enough to get her from the bus to the
station wagon to the house to a bed in the dark. Besides, Miss
Candy, as she called the woman in later years, would not
push talk. She mostly made statements about herself, then
stopped, giving you plenty of room and time to breathe.

They were standing in the field. A medium shot with hot
light. Jewel, tall with squarish shoulders and athletic calves,
was pulling the brim of her denim cap down and using both
hands to shade her eyes. Miss Candy, dainty but sinewy and
solid, never hid from weather of any kind. She stood with her
arms slightly bent, her hands sliding off her hips. The ground
was plowed up to receive the rain deeply should it ever

come, Miss Candy explained, turning toward the sheds to show her granddaughter all that she had done with the family farm, giving the younger woman time to steer them to the conversation she had traveled from New York to have.

"It's been waiting for a long time, it would seem," said Jewel, running a hand across the bark of the tree Miss Candy had planted on the day of Jewel's christening. "Rain'll come in time. It's a good tree," she'd said as if it were a causal thing.

Miss Candy stooped to the earth and traced the travels of the tree roots barely bulging beneath the bristly grass. "A good woman does not rot," she said on her haunches like some ancient sage. "But slow-ass men can certainly let her get overripe," Jewel added.

Miss Candy tilted her head up to laugh at that a long while. Then they went into the house, holding each other round. The Franklin stove had been moved to the living room, so they sat before it and sprawled the album out before them. Miss Candy's first husband was the doctor. And while she waited for him to get through school, she earned her midwife certificate, taught elocution, discovered she was sterile, and took over the family farm for the first time. Climbing into bed with that one, she'd say, was like climbing into bed with a dining-room set. They'd married in the great stone church standing still at the crossroads. He had died shortly after, and all the family thought Miss Candy, or M'Dear as she was then, would stay boarded up in the house forever. But then she went back to giving elocution lessons and midwiving around the countryside. Twenty years later Willie Dupree pranced into town. Fly, they called him. Fast Foot, Cool Breeze, Willie Wail. She called him Honey. He called her Miss Candy. They were married in a fever, is how she said it, pointing to the two wedding pictures side by side. The first, stiff and posed and sober. The other, a close-up of two smiling faces, so close you could see the love flowers on her neck as though a vampire had leapt from the shutter.

Miss Candy had laughed at that notion, going on to say that Honey was just the sort of crazy man you'd gladly dance over the cliff with. Only he'd danced away and with someone else and no cliff in sight. And she'd turned the farm over to the Caroline cousins, converted the station wagon into a caravan, and took to the road for several years mending pots and sharpening blades and winding up in New England.

"And Paul?" she asked finally, for that of course was why she had played out the scene of sharing her memories. "That man very much takes his own sweet time."

"He's very dedicated," Jewel had mustered in his defense. "There's so much work to be done . . . before we can make . . . our arrangements."

"And while you're ripening," Miss Candy had smiled, "how's the work?"

"New play in the fall. The movie rights have been sold and I might get to play . . ." She had not wanted to get into that. She had wanted to speak of other things, things one spoke of in the the kitchen while getting your hair braided, while someone made biscuits and commented from time to time, while the radio was on "Wings Over Jordan" and the conversation was put on hold when one of your favorites came on. But family ties no longer knitted close and there was no one to say let's get our wagons in a circle when someone was in crisis. So she'd come to M'Dear, Miss Candy, the last of that generation who believed in sustaining, and come to speak about this man and his distances. She wanted to tell her about the years of penance as he forgave piece by piece

lying there sweaty, her legs still in a tremble, the nipples still erect, she felt him moving away, traveling great distances. When just moments before they'd jumped the waves, and no undertow, no drowning, no dangers on release. For the first time in a long time he was not dying or forgiving or

104

*withholding, but loving her and giving himself over to plea-
sure. Just a split second ago she had felt him against her
again and touched him then felt him retreating, the arm
muscle flexed under her back, alert for ambush, then flabby,
then gone. He rolled over and switched on the radio and
disappeared into the music. She snuggled against his back
and tried to tangle her legs in his. And he became a Chinese
box*

The man helped her off the bus and deposited her suitcase by the mailbox of the town square. Jewel looked around.
It was a huge open space, silenced and static and ready for
snow. The trees, rid of their rags now, were naked, awaiting
assault. It would be gusting soon. Miss Candy's station wagon
was nowhere in sight. And the stores were closed for the
evening. In panic, she felt a leaking somewhere. There
seemed to be no space on the inside to pause and let the mind
locate the spring. She stared hard at the pavement. My water
broke, she told herself, my bladder. And then she fixed the
area as her face. She sniffed. She couldn't be sure whether it
was the nose or the eyes. She put her mind instead to assem-
bling words again for Miss Candy. She would want to know
first and foremost about the accident. Jewel couldn't concen-
trate. She was still leaking somewhere, like a too-quick
douche that leaves you gurgling in your pants all day. But
that couldn't be it. She looked around. In the open air, she
mused, there is room for the awful if there is room of any
kind at all. She turned her good side to the solitary figure who
had turned the far corner, flinging salt from a pail like a
farmer. She watched him out of the side of her eye, wondering if he could feel the heat, wondering if she beamed hard
enough, whether she could turn him around and he'd come
running to gather her up in his pail.

"Jewel." As though she had just decided on the suitable
name for the baby that first time as the elders recounted it.

Miss Candy was leaning over and rolling the window down. Jewel struggled in and kissed the old woman and they sat back to look at each other. Jewel was fatter than usual and kind of wide-open around the eyes that seemed dangerously bright. Miss Candy seemed to have gotten smaller, or maybe just swallowed up in the plaid alpaca that had been Dupree's at some point in his fishing time, for the holes and snares and tears were fishhooks and keys and tools at five o'clock in the morning and too sleepy to care. Jewel remembered suddenly that she had liked Honey Dupree very much. He and Paul had gone fishing once and gotten drunk and come back soaking-wet and loud.

"You brought an autumn snow with you, I see, Jewel," she smiled, taking off slowly and making a point of showing she was being careful with her passenger.

No one, it seemed, was preparing for a gale or snowstorm. Even the big fishing boats were still hauling, the old Portagees swaying over the side to yank at a net or a casket of wine. Miss Candy's yawl, bobbing and straining against its threadbare moorings, was not even pulled up to shore, much less put up for the season. Bad William, Miss Candy's partner in the grinder shop, was out past the wharf, balancing on a clutter of rocks and singing as always. Too far to call, too cold to roll the window down, too tired to care, Jewel simply smiled at the memory of him standing in the doorway of Miss Candy's house, big and clumsy with his hands, introducing himself as just her partner less the woman he regarded as young and ladylike think ill of his presence.

Miss Candy pulled into the yard and Jewel felt the car sink into the gravel. She watched Bad William's attempts with his gear. He heaved the traps off the rocks again and again, retrieving the trap, wet and rusty, the white chunk of bait flying between the wires with every heave like a mad bird banging to be free to fly up over them and carry off the roof of the station wagon. Miss Candy beeped and Bad William let the trap slide off the side of the rocks and sink below. He waved back, but his hand seemed too close, like through a fish-eye lens of a new order, as if it would smash through the windshield.

"I need to fill in this driveway some more," said Miss Candy.

"Yes, for some time now the ground keeps caving in . . ."

The old woman turned in her seat, then decided the station wagon was close enough to the house where it was.

When she awoke she was under an afghan, one corner familiar, for it had been her baby carriage cover. Something noisy was cooking in the fireplace, a duck maybe, something greasy at any rate. Miss Candy was stretched out on the couch opposite, sipping sherry, a bowl of cranberries in her lap, a magazine curled on her chest.

"You were certainly done in," she said. "How are you feeling?" She directed Jewel's eyes to the aluminum cart in the kitchen doorway, mysterious under the white sheeting, but not mysterious at all. The woman was ready.

Jewel nodded and felt her eyes fall off the woman. She couldn't quite keep her in focus. She kept changing age or something, and color too, like a revolving filter was attached to the camera eye. On the hard-swept floors were the rag rugs she had helped Miss Candy sew the winter Paul had gone off to edit their first film together. It was the time Miss Candy had suggested that someone in the household could use a psychiatrist, a witchdoctor is how she'd joked it. Jewel had made an effort after that to relate more clearly just what madness existed in her home, asking for advice. And Miss Candy had shrugged and said there was nothing for Jewel to win. And Jewel busied herself with threading needles and sticking them into the cushion so Miss Candy would not have to slow up her work. And she'd resolved to move out of the house, for the tension was rotting her life, and there was simply no good reason for them to continue plundering each other. But she'd gone home and she'd stayed. It seemed a waste to have spent that winter with Miss Candy, studying the script only to junk it all. And it was a good film.

"I still remember the reviews," Miss Candy said, meeting her eyes coming up off the rugs. "Every reviewer wrote of you as though you were their own personal discovery. Like you hadn't been out there scuffling all these years. Hmph, as if cream no longer rises to the top. 'Her performance possessed moments of diabolic power,' was how one paper put it. And just think, Jewel, somewhere right now some writer is dreaming you up the new part. And somewhere else they're just now casting the Oscar that—"

Jewel heard herself laughing. This was the most she had ever known Miss Candy to speak all at once. She seemed younger somehow than the last few times she had seen her. That was good. She would need steady, sure hands when the baby burst her open. Jewel tunneled under the afghan while Miss Candy talked on. If I can just locate the—she searched for "geological" and that took some time—geological stairway, I might be able to get deep down, landing by landing, layer by layer, uncovering the layers of secrets stashed away in mothballs that won't stay folded, layers and layers down to the nerve-lined pit of black to dig for richness with my fingers and find a someone there who's been rummaging through the trunks and caves and knows all the terrible hurts that haven't cracked through to the surface and been revealed in the close-ups damning her, and she'd ask, Is there madness in me, have you stumbled upon any sign of—

"You look flushed," Miss Candy said, suddenly there with a hand approaching her forehead. *Jewel felt Paul's hand on her spine, him telling her that if she could get the body to make the statement they could cut the lines out all together, for she was fumbling them anyway. His hand on her spine to feel the contraction, and she forcing the blood to rush there for a good rehearsal at least, no matter what she did after when he moved away.* "It's natural enough to be feverish at this time, but don't worry, you're in good hands," Miss Candy patted. *But when he stepped away and called for the contraction again to be sure it was visible at a distance, she felt a constriction in the spine that was not voluntary. And then he was behind the first cameraman, and she felt it again at the base of her back as if some natural growth was being first stifled then strangled. Bound and gagged she struggled through the scene and when he called finish, disgusted, she had ripped off the dress right on the spot, trying to explain about the tyranny of the cloth she'd been forced to wear as though it were the dressmaker's fault her spine was paralyzed and the several layers of splendid costumes just beneath the skin were being shredded. Of course she had gone on much too long about it. And he had laughed that laugh. The laugh they all laughed which meant if you weren't careful you would be destroyed. Then he told her her pacing was off, erratic, lousy. And she'd answered that pacing was a director's duty and the editor's craft. That's what triggered off the argument in the car. And why she was in the back seat (thinking on this rhythm, for the past few months she was being propelled by a rhythm other than her own. As if a malaria parasite was clocking her body to its own reproductive cycles. And she'd been dumb enough to think this out with the mouth open. And he had told her that he'd been right in the first place. She should've gotten rid of the kid in the beginning. It was driving her crazier than she already was and it was ruining his work). Which is why he hadn't kept his eyes on the road.*

"Tell me something, Jewel," said Miss Candy, perching herself on the edge of the couch so she was in profile and not looking at her. "Why did you stay on with him after so long?"

Jewel squeezed her eyes shut and searched her head for room to lay the words out so she could select carefully. How to explain that she could be the matter on which his mysterious energy could play. Radio waves were unperceived but for a suitable instrument to catch them up and transform them to something sensible. She got hold of "sensible" and decided it meant something else and what a pity. She searched her brain again, like an instrument to detect, record, snatch and reflect the energies that that

"Like I said to Cathy—you know she was always pulling her hair out over you and Paul, she worships you, her Aunt Jewel the movie star—when a woman lives with a man for ten years she is not being abused. You understand what I'm saying, yes?"

Jewel examined the parchment face in profile, foxed like a first edition, the head a lean affair carrying the line of the cheekbone up, the tightly braided rows of dark etched onto the scalp and barely visible in this light, the neck thin and sloping, rising up out of dainty shoulders that almost weren't there, one arm bent with the fragile stemware now empty. The other arm, Jewel discovered, was across her, the hand on the mound rising up straight in front of her mouth. It seemed as if a furnace had fallen on her. And why had she come to this place when what she wanted was to be far from gravity and tides and words and states of emergencies and no longer open to suggestion.

"How do you feel . . . about it all? You mustn't blame yourself. People always do of course. That's what it means to be the survivor. But . . . I could use something to eat. Maybe you should just have a little soup for now." She patted the legs bunched up under the afghan. "I'm so glad you've come. I was expecting you right after . . . months ago. No one knew where you were for so long a time." Miss Candy stretched to capacity to kiss her granddaughter, who was barely available above the woolen wrap.

Jewel followed Miss Candy around the room. In one light she looked like salami. Bending to the fireplace with the dishes and fork, she looked like a wizened dwarf. The glint from her earrings shone like a side eye. Jewel forced an intake of air and tried to give herself over to the aromas. There was some sloshing in the pot. She would not eat the soup. It would be simple enough to just set it aside. There was clinking of metal. She waited to hear the woman set the grinder wheel in motion. But instead she heard a car-horn sound and not too far away. Then blobs of light streaking through the front drapes. Miss Candy went to the window and Jewel thought she detected a sinister grin.

"It's Cathy," she said turning. And it was Miss Candy again, M'Dear, Other Mother as the young nieces and nephews called her, no one else. Jewel tried to get to her feet. You had to be on your feet to deal with Cathy. She wasn't sure she was up to it. The strident clothes, the face sealed over in pancake, the breastplate jewelry. She had to be beaten, bruised and screamed at to reach. Jewel always felt compelled to grab her by her ears and scream hard into them, the mouth, the nose, to get to the person buried below under all the metallic sheeting and cloth and greasy cement that just vaguely let the features through but didn't seem to affect the voice box any. She had seen Cathy last, not counting the funeral, which was a sudden five-minute notice, and she'd seen no one there but Paul, who seemed older and with much more gray hair than she remembered in real life, and she stood there joking about Dorian Gray till she realized she was talking out loud and then the fit and the diving under the flowers for cover but gagging, a week before the accident she'd seen her. Their anniversary actually, which Cathy had staged as a surprise. Which it was.

There were ghosts in the kitchen. She had stumbled in aware of some night visitation that would reveal its purpose

*if she could wait. A clump of dishtowel stuff was by the door,
and she wiped her feet automatically and shuffled over the
sugar, gritty by the sink, past the table tumbled down with
cloudy glasses. Bits of this and that were on the greasy stove.
Her head was itching, scratching it produced blobs of greasy
dye under the fingernails which she flicked and wiped on her
bathrobe. Pumped to her mouth suddenly were last night's
poor choices and she raced to the sink and banged too hard
and got scared, looking down at an elbow or a knee, poking
her navel out. She couldn't get close enough to the sink or in
time.*

*"Damn, baby," he said, moving into the kitchen, mean-
ing the kitchen. "Oh shit," he said, meaning the smell. "It
gets worse and worse. Other women don't have morning
sickness twenty-four hours around the clock every day of the
year. Oh no," as she turned to face him, the vomit plastered
down the front of the bathrobe. He backed out of the kitchen,
yelling from the bathroom that he was going to stay at a
hotel for a few nights cause his nerves were shot. And she
found herself leaning on the breadknife, asking the arbiter
below her ballooning breasts if she may take the giant step.*

Cathy had come in late afternoon and found her in the
bathrobe, huddled on the window-seat.

"Look, sugar, you're going to have to get your shit together better than this. Your door was wide open. The house
is a mess. You're a horror. The baby ain't shaping up nearly
as fat as your breasts and chins are. And you're putting Paul
through a whole lotta unnecessary shit. He just called me
from the Hotel Albert to come over here and get things in
order and I certainly—"

"Please stop talking."

"Say wha?"

"Just shut up. Finally."

"Look," coming closer and motioning her to get out of the

bathrobe as she took off her coat and threw her bag on the couch. "I'll gladly do the laundry and clean the house and shampoo your hair and deal with that atrocity tale you're wearing, but I am not about to shut up. And I will tell you why." She stood over Jewel and took the bathrobe by the nape of its neck and held it dangling. "What you need is a reality tester. What you got is a hard head and a niece who loves you. Now, didn't I stand by you when you decided to have this baby, cause you need something of your own to love, right? So I'm entitled to run my mouth a little. And what I want to say is this. You gotta get out of here. You can come stay with me till after the baby and you decide what to do. It's killing both of you whatever it is. And it's dumb cause you both such groovy people. O.K. I'm extreme, I admit it. Best way to solve problems, I always thought, was abandon them. Know what I mean? Like there was this story that got hold of me when I was little—"

"Please shut up."

"Somebody makes a pot of coffee or maybe it was a stew, no matter. And they put in salt instead of sugar. So they don't know what to do. So—"

"You don't put sugar—"

"So some bright person suggests they dump some cracked eggshells in to absorb the salt. But then the egg shells turn a funny color. Like unedible-looking. So some other Einstein decides on some kerosene which will color—"

Jewel pressed up against the window. She could see the pavement below still wet from the rain. Cathy was moving about the room dumping ashtrays into a paper bag and fluffing up pillows and talking talking talking.

"So they wind up with this terrible mess of eggshells and car tires and bicycle chains and whatnot and they're tearing their hair out as to how to turn this into a good stew or pot of coffee or whatever it was supposed to be, I forget. So someone with half a brain says they should call in the lady from Philadelphia. Or the lady from Mali in some versions, depending on what folks are printing the book. And the lady strolls in with her umbrella and Red Cross shoes and dumps the shit out the back door and sets a fresh pot of water on to boil."

"And you are the lady from Philadelphia?"

"And I'm here to tell you that you are losing your mind and have to get out of here." She had gone into the kitchen now and was banging around with the pots on the stove. Jewel half expected a coffeepot with snow tires to be cooked up. She had to admit she felt better. She would get up and help. "And another thing," said Cathy coming back with a dishtowel. "Hey, you look weird, Jewel." Jewel felt something erupting hot and acid and churning. She leaned away from the window and tried to get up and tripped over her slipper, dragging the dishtowel out of Cathy's hands.

Within minutes, the candelabra went skidding across the flagstone, banging the seltzer bottles down like bowling pins. Teddy has a penchant for dying off banisters as you know, Cathy, so we killed him many times, sometimes running him through and dumping him over the banister from above, sometimes conking him over the head with the battle-ax from the iron man standing on the landing, then shoving him over the banister toward the piano. Sometimes we hoisted him on to the chandelier so he could catapult over the rail. The bear, though, was a bit dodgy at first. One of the youngsters, or maybe just a dwarf under contract from before and now no work of that kind, had stomped both eyes out. And the teeth were yellow and needed touching up, plus the bald spots. But the make-up man said he was an expert on toupee jobs. Oh yes, there was an egg in attendance. A large egg. It wasn't in the script. Matter of fact, none of this was in the script they gave me. They do that to you sometimes to show contempt. So you can't keep up. I didn't bat an eye.

So this egg, like I was saying. So large that the cameramen had to break it up into a thousand million

"Cathy's here," Miss Candy announced, going to the door.

Jewel got to her feet at last and had just enough time to fluff her hair where the pillows had mashed it when Cathy came in behind bushels and bushels of those flowers. Jewel heard someone screaming and saw Miss Candy run toward her as she was running out.

Patches of open water persisted beyond the pilings, steel-gray and blue, pieces breaking off to float from the ice, resisting the freeze. Icicles hung from the underside of the wharf, a ghostly skirt dripping onto the ice below, pockmarking the surface. Jewel untied the yawl, the whiskered knot giving in crackles. Pushing off, her back to the ocean, she could see the family next door to Bad Williams' building a fire in the yard, burning old spade handles and last summer's bait baskets. "Winter is icumen in," she sang, and tugged at the motor's starter string. The charred and sooty heaps were blowing apart, gusting out of the yard and down past the wharf, streaking gray marks across the frozen surface. From this angle, she thought, I could skip stones clear across to Miss Candy's window. She turned to meet the water ahead where it was open and the strength of the water broke up the log jams of ice, leaving dead gulls to pitch and bob on their frosty beds.

She threw her leg over the side and was not surprised to find the water was not cold at all, warm in fact, like late summer. She cocked both cameras and steadied them on the seat beside her. She was out beyond the old mill now, only faintly heard the weird music in the rafters, and just barely seen some hairy something or others hardened on the shelves that the blades of snow made. She faced around again and took up one of the cameras. The dunes were snow castles. She shot it.

"I'd like to listen to you, Cathy. You've always given sound advice, M'Dear. But I am some other mother's rambling polar bear and we simply do not swim in similar pools." She shot the boat seat, the spot she'd just relinquished when she stood up.

Steadily, slowly, she hooked up the time attachment on the other camera, stooping, elevated it with the camera case. Then slowly up again to strip, stooping again to ease herself over the side. Counting the final wink as the camera whizzed, then release to the water, the last three fingers pause, then are gone. The water is warm. Hot, in fact. But she hadn't counted on the pain. The pain that burrowed up under her tongue and pulled at the roots of her teeth, her hair, her vagina. That wrenched the hinges off her thighs and pulled her anus inside out. She was moving every which way and all at once, There'd be sharks. But she couldn't gather enough of herself to go in one direction and avoid them. There'd be rocks. Unamenable things at the bottom to tear her and make her bleed. And there'll never be blood enough to make her clean.

"Don't push any more, sugar, just breathe, just breathe."

"Pant, Jewel. Pant, pant, pant, dammit." Miss Candy gave her knee a hard knock. "I said to pant now. Talk quickly. Anything. Pant."

"Lord iam notworthy lordiam notworthy lordam notworthit."

"Wasn't she having contractions, Miss Candy?"

"She never said a word. Numb, I think. I felt only mild thumps and pulls."

"Damn, I came just in time."

"None of us ever come in time," said Miss Cathy.

Jewel didn't let on she was awake and spying. She watched the ancient dwarf pull the creature glistening with seaweed out of her left thigh. She watched them smile at the thing and then at her. The smile that meant if you didn't plan carefully, you would be destroyed. It was best to play the scene out with a few lines and bide her time. The dwarf now had metamorphosed into a salami, but she was fooling no one. A salami can be sliced. And she'd come to the right house for sharp blades for the job. As for the metallic monster in the mud encasing, there was always dynamite. She'd have to empty her head to get some room for something befitting the sea urchin now howling for her blood.

Sweet
Town

*I*T IS HARD TO BELIEVE that there was only one spring and one summer apiece that year, my fifteenth year. It is hard to believe that I so quickly squandered my youth in the sweet town playground of the sunny city, that wild monkeybardom of my fourth-grade youthhood. However, it was so.

"Dear Mother"—I wrote one day on her bathroom mirror with a candle sliver—"please forgive my absence and my decay and overlook the freckled dignity and pockmarked integrity plaguing me this season."

I used to come on even wilder sometimes and write her mad cryptic notes on the kitchen sink with charred matches. Anything for a bit, we so seldom saw each other. I even sometimes wrote her a note on paper. And then one day, having romped my soul through the spectrum of sunny colors, I dashed up to her apartment to escape the heat and found a letter from her which eternally elated my heart to the point of bursture and generally endeared her to me forever. Written on the kitchen table in cake frosting was the message, "My dear, mad, perverse young girl, kindly take care and paint the fire escape in your leisure . . ." All the *i*'s were dotted with marmalade, the *t*'s were crossed with orange rind. Here was a sight to carry with one forever in the back of the screaming eyeballs somewhere. I howled for at least five minutes out of sheer madity and vowed to love her completely. Leisure. As if bare-armed spring ever let up from its invitation to perpetuate the race. And as if we ever owned a fire escape. "Zweep," I yelled, not giving a damn for intelligibility and decided that if ever I was to run away from home, I'd take her with me. And with that in mind, and with Penelope splintering through the landscape and the pores secreting animal champagne, I bent my youth to the season's tempo and proceeded to lose my mind.

There is a certain glandular disturbance all beautiful, wizardy, great people have second sight to, that trumpets through the clothes, sets the nerves up for the kill, and torments the senses to orange explosure. It has something to do with the cosmic interrelationship between the cellular atunement of certain designated organs and the firmental correlation with the axis shifts of the globe. My mother calls it sex and my brother says it's groin-fever time. But then, they were always ones for brevity. Anyway, that's the way it was. And in this spring race, the glands always win and the muses and the brain core must step aside to ride in the trunk with the spare tire. It was during this sweet and drugged madness time that I met B. J., wearing his handsomeness like an article of clothing, for an effect, and wearing his friend Eddie like a necessary pimple of adolescence. It was on the beach that we met, me looking great in a pair of cut-off dungarees and them with beards. Never mind the snows of yesteryear, I told myself, I'll take the sand and sun blizzard any day.

"Listen, Kit," said B. J. to me one night after we had experienced such we-encounters with the phenomenal world at large as a two-strawed mocha, duo-jaywalking summons, twosome whistling scenes, and other such like we-experiences, "the thing for us to do is hitch to the Coast and get into films."

"Righto," said Ed. "And soon."

"Sure thing, honeychile," I said, and jumped over an unknown garbage can. "We were made for celluloid—beautifully chiseld are we, not to mention well-buffed." I ran up and down somebody's stoop, whistling "Columbia the Gem of the Ocean" through my nose. And Eddie made siren sounds and walked a fence. B. J. grasped a parking-sign pole and extended himself parallel to the ground. I applauded, not only the gymnastics but also the offer. We liked to make bold directionless overtures to action like those crazy teenagers you're always running into on the printed page or MGM movies.

"We could buy a sleeping bag," said B. J., and challenged a store cat to duel.

"We could buy a sleeping bag," echoed Eddie, who never had any real contribution to make in the say of statements.

"Three in a bag," I said while B. J. grasped me by the belt and we went flying down a side street. "Hrumph," I coughed, and perched on a fire hydrant. "Only one bag?"

"Of course," said B. J.

"Of course," said Ed. "And hrumph."

We came on like this the whole summer, even crazier. All of our friends abandoned us, they couldn't keep the pace. My mother threatened me with disinheritance. And my old roommate from camp actually turned the hose on me one afternoon in a fit of Florence Nightingale therapy. But hand in hand, me and Pan, and Eddie too, whizzed through the cement kaleidoscope making our own crazy patterns, singing our own song. And then one night a crazy thing happened. I dreamt that B. J. was running down the street howling, tearing his hair out and making love to the garbage cans on the boulevard. I was there laughing my head off and Eddie was spinning a beer bottle with a faceless person I didn't even know. I woke up and screamed for no reason I know of and my roommate, who was living with us, threw a Saltine cracker at me in way of saying something about silence, peace, consideration, and sleepdom. And then on top of that another crazy thing happened. Pebbles were flying into my opened window. The whole thing struck me funny. It wasn't a casement window and there was no garden underneath. I naturally laughed my head off and my roommate got really angry and cursed me out viciously. I explained to her that pebbles were coming in, but she wasn't one for imagination and turned over into sleepdom. I went to the window to see who I was going to share my balcony scene with, and there below, standing on the milkbox, was B. J. I climbed out and joined him on the stoop.

"What's up?" I asked, ready to take the world by storm in my mixed-match baby-doll pajamas. B. J. motioned me into the foyer and I could see by the distraught mask that he was wearing that serious discussion was afoot.

"Listen, Kit," he began, looking both ways with unnecessary caution. "We're leaving, tonight, now. Me and Eddie. He stole some money from his grandmother, so we're cutting out."

"Where're ya going?" I asked. He shrugged. And just then I saw Eddie dash across the stoop and into the shadows. B. J. shrugged and he made some kind of desperate sound with his voice like a stifled cry. "It's been real great. The summer and you . . . but . . ."

"Look here," I said with anger. "I don't know why the hell you want to hang around with that nothing." I was really angry but sorry too. It wasn't at all what I wanted to say. I would have liked to have said, "Apollo, we are the only beautiful people in the world. And because our genes are so great, our kid can't help but burst through the human skin into cosmic significance." I wanted to say, "You will bear in mind that I am great, brilliant, talented, good-looking, and am going to college at fifteen. I have the most interesting complexes ever, and despite Freud and Darwin I have made

a healthy adjustment as an earthworm." But I didn't tell him
this. Instead, I revealed that petty, small, mean side of me by
saying "Eddie is a shithead."

B. J. scratched his head, swung his foot in an arc, groaned
and took off. "Maybe next summer . . ." he started to say but
his voice cracked and he and Eddie went dashing down the
night street, arm in arm. I stood there with my thighs bare
and my soul shook. Maybe we will meet next summer, I told
the mailboxes. Or maybe I'll quit school and bum around the
country. And in every town I'll ask for them as the hotel
keeper feeds the dusty, weary traveler that I'll be. "Have you
seen two guys, one great, the other acned? If you see 'em, tell
'em Kit's looking for them." And I'd bandage up my cactus-
torn feet and sling the knapsack into place and be off. And
in the next town, having endured dust storms, tornadoes,
earthquakes, and coyotes, I'll stop at the saloon and inquire.
"Yeh, they travel together," I'd say in a voice somewhere
between W. C. Fields and Gladys Cooper. "Great buddies.
Inseparable. Tell 'em for me that Kit's still a great kid."

And legends'll pop up about me and my quest. Great long
twelve-bar blues ballads with eighty-nine stanzas. And a
strolling minstrel will happen into the feedstore where B. J.'ll
be and hear and shove the farmer's daughter off his lap and
mount up to find me. Or maybe we won't meet ever, or we
will but I won't recognize him cause he'll be an enchanted
frog or a bald-headed fat man and I'll be God knows what.
No matter. Days other than the here and now, I told myself,
will be dry and sane and sticky with the rotten apricots ooz-
ing slowly in the sweet time of my betrayed youth.

Blues
Ain't
No
Mockin
Bird

*T*HE PUDDLE HAD FROZEN OVER, and me and Cathy went stompin in it. The twins from next door, Tyrone and Terry, were swingin so high out of sight we forgot we were waitin our turn on the tire. Cathy jumped up and came down hard on her heels and started tap-dancin. And the frozen patch splinterin every which way underneath kinda spooky. "Looks like a plastic spider web," she said. "A sort of weird spider, I guess, with many mental problems." But really it looked like the crystal paperweight Granny kept in the parlor. She was on the back porch, Granny was, making the cakes drunk. The old ladle dripping rum into the Christmas tins, like it used to drip maple syrup into the pails when we lived in the Judson's woods, like it poured cider into the vats when we were on the Cooper place, like it used to scoop buttermilk and soft cheese when we lived at the dairy.

"Go tell that man we ain't a bunch of trees."

"Ma'am?"

"I said to tell that man to get away from here with that camera." Me and Cathy look over toward the meadow where the men with the station wagon'd been roamin around all mornin. The tall man with a huge camera lassoed to his shoulder was buzzin our way.

129

"They're makin movie pictures," yelled Tyrone, stiffenin his legs and twistin so the tire'd come down slow so they could see.

"They're makin movie pictures," sang out Terry.

"That boy don't never have anything original to say," say Cathy grown-up.

By the time the man with the camera had cut across our neighbor's yard, the twins were out of the trees swingin low and Granny was onto the steps, the screen door bammin soft and scratchy against her palms. "We thought we'd get a shot or two of the house and everything and then—"

"Good mornin," Granny cut him off. And smiled that smile.

"Good mornin," he said, head all down the way Bingo does when you yell at him about the bones on the kitchen floor. "Nice place you got here, aunty. We thought we'd take a—"

"Did you?" said Granny with her eyebrows. Cathy pulled up her socks and giggled.

"Nice things here," said the man, buzzin his camera over the yard. The pecan barrels, the sled, me and Cathy, the flowers, the printed stones along the driveway, the trees, the twins, the toolshed.

"I don't know about the thing, the it, and the stuff," said Granny, still talkin with her eyebrows. "Just people here is what I tend to consider."

Camera man stopped buzzin. Cathy giggled into her collar.

"Mornin, ladies," a new man said. He had come up behind us when we weren't lookin. "And gents," discoverin the twins givin him a nasty look. "We're filmin for the county," he said with a smile. "Mind if we shoot a bit around here?"

"I do indeed," said Granny with no smile. Smilin man was smiling up a storm. So was Cathy. But he didn't seem to have another word to say, so he and the camera man backed on out the yard, but you could hear the camera buzzin still. "Suppose you just shut that machine off," said Granny real low through her teeth, and took a step down off the porch and then another.

"Now, aunty," Camera said, pointin the thing straight at her.

"Your mama and I are not related."

Smilin man got his notebook out and a chewed-up pencil. "Listen," he said movin back into our yard, "we'd like to have a statement from you . . . for the film. We're filmin for the county, see. Part of the food stamp campaign. You know about the food stamps?"

Granny said nuthin.

"Maybe there's somethin you want to say for the film. I see you grow your own vegetables," he smiled real nice. "If more folks did that, see, there'd be no need—"

Granny wasn't sayin nuthin. So they backed on out, buzzin at our clothesline and the twins' bicycles, then back on down to the meadow. The twins were danglin in the tire, lookin at Granny. Me and Cathy were waitin, too, cause Granny always got somethin to say. She teaches steady with no let-up "I was on this bridge one time," she started off. "Was a crowd cause this man was goin to jump, you understand. And a minister was there and the police and some other folks. His woman was there, too."

"What was they doin?" asked Tyrone.

"Tryin to talk him out of it was what they was doin. The minister talkin about how it was a mortal sin, suicide. His woman takin bites out of her own hand and not even knowin it, so nervous and cryin and talkin fast."

"So what happened?" asked Tyrone.

"So here comes . . . this person . . . with a camera, takin pictures of the man and the minister and the woman. Takin pictures of the man in his misery about to jump, cause life so bad and people been messin with him so bad. This person takin up the whole roll of film practically. But savin a few, of course."

"Of course," said Cathy, hatin the person. Me standin there wonderin how Cathy knew it was "of course" when I didn't and it was *my* grandmother.

After a while Tyrone say, "Did he jump?"

"Yeh, did he jump?" say Terry all eager.

And Granny just stared at the twins till their faces swallow up the eager and they don't even care any more about the man jumpin. Then she goes back onto the porch and lets the screen door go for itself. I'm lookin to Cathy to finish the story cause she knows Granny's whole story before me even. Like she knew how come we move so much and Cathy ain't but a third cousin we picked up on the way last Thanksgivin visitin. But she knew it was on account of people drivin Granny crazy till she'd get up in the night and start packin. Mumblin and packin and wakin everybody up sayin, "Let's get on away from here before I kill me somebody." Like people wouldn't pay her for things like they said they would. Or Mr. Judson bringin us boxes of old clothes and raggedy magazines. Or Mrs. Cooper comin in our kitchen and touchin everything and sayin how clean it all was. Granny goin crazy, and Granddaddy Cain pullin her off the people, sayin, "Now, now, Cora." But next day loadin up the truck, with rocks all in his jaw, madder than Granny in the first place.

"I read a story once," said Cathy soundin like Granny teacher. "About this lady Goldilocks who barged into a house that wasn't even hers. And not invited, you understand. Messed over the people's groceries and broke up the people's furniture. Had the nerve to sleep in the folks' bed."

"Then what happened?" asked Tyrone. "What they do, the folks, when they come in to all this mess?"

"Did they make her pay for it?" asked Terry, makin a first. "I'd've made her pay me."

I didn't even ask. I could see Cathy actress was very likely to just walk away and leave us in mystery about this story which I heard was about some bears.

"Did they throw her out?" asked Tyrone, like his father sounds when he's bein extra nasty-plus to the washin-machine man.

"Woulda," said Terry. "I woulda gone upside her head with my fist and—"

"You woulda done whatcha always do—go cry to Mama, you big baby," said Tyrone. So naturally Terry starts hittin on Tyrone, and next thing you know they tumblin out the tire and rollin on the ground. But Granny didn't say a thing or send the twins home or step out on the steps to tell us about how we can't afford to be fightin amongst ourselves. She didn't say nuthin. So I get into the tire to take my turn. And I could see her leanin up against the pantry table, starin at the cakes she was puttin up for the Christmas sale, mumblin real low and grumpy and holdin her forehead like it wanted to fall off and mess up the rum cakes.

Behind me I hear before I can see Granddaddy Cain comin through the woods in his field boots. Then I twist around to see the shiny black oilskin cuttin through what little left there was of yellows, reds, and oranges. His great white head not quite round cause of this bloody thing high on his shoulder, like he was wearin a cap on sideways. He takes the shortcut through the pecan grove, and the sound of twigs snapping overhead and underfoot travels clear and cold all the way up to us. And here comes Smilin and Camera up behind him like they was goin to do somethin. Folks like to go for him sometimes. Cathy say it's because he's so tall and quiet and like a king. And people just can't stand it. But Smilin and Camera don't hit him in the head or nuthin. They just buzz on him as he stalks by with the chicken hawk slung over his shoulder, squawkin, drippin red down the back of the oilskin. He passes the porch and stops a second for Granny to see he's caught the hawk at last, but she's just starin and mumblin, and not at the hawk. So he nails the bird to the toolshed door, the hammerin crackin through the eardrums. And the bird flappin himself to death and droolin down the door to paint the gravel in the driveway red, then brown, then black. And the two men movin up on tiptoe like they was invisible or we were blind, one.

"Get them persons out of my flower bed, Mister Cain," say Granny moanin real low like at a funeral.

"How come your grandmother calls her husband 'Mister Cain' all the time?" Tyrone whispers all loud and noisy and from the city and don't know no better. Like his mama, Miss Myrtle, tell us never mind the formality as if we had no better breeding than to call her Myrtle, plain. And then this awful thing—a giant hawk—come wailin up over the meadow, flyin low and tilted and screamin, zigzaggin through the pecan grove, breakin branches and hollerin, snappin past the clothesline, flyin every which way, flyin into things reckless with crazy.

"He's come to claim his mate," say Cathy fast, and ducks down. We all fall quick and flat into the gravel driveway, stones scrapin my face. I squinch my eyes open again at the hawk on the door, tryin to fly up out of her death like it was just a sack flown into by mistake. Her body holdin her there on that nail, though. The mate beatin the air overhead and clutchin for hair, for heads, for landin space.

The camera man duckin and bendin and runnin and fallin, jigglin the camera and scared. And Smilin jumpin up and down swipin at the huge bird, tryin to bring the hawk down with just his raggedy ole cap. Granddaddy Cain straight up and silent, watchin the circles of the hawk, then aimin the hammer off his wrist. The giant bird fallin, silent and slow. Then here comes Camera and Smilin all big and bad now that the awful screechin thing is on its back and broken, here they come. And Granddaddy Cain looks up at them like it was the first time noticin, but not payin them too much mind cause he's listenin, we all listenin, to that low groanin music comin from the porch. And we figure any minute, somethin in my back tells me any minute now, Granny gonna bust through that screen with somethin in her hand and murder on her mind. So Granddaddy say above the buzzin, but quiet, "Good day, gentlemen." Just like that. Like he'd invited them in to play cards and they'd stayed too long and all the sandwiches were gone and Reverend Webb was droppin by and it was time to go.

They didn't know what to do. But like Cathy say, folks can't stand Granddaddy tall and silent and like a king. They can't neither. The smile the men smilin is pullin the mouth back and showin the teeth. Lookin like the wolf man, both of them. Then Grandaddy holds his hand out— this huge hand I used to sit in when I was a baby and he'd carry me through the house to my mother like I was a gift on a tray. Like he used to on the trains. They called the other men just waiters. But they spoke of Granddaddy separate and said, The Waiter. And said he had engines in his feet and motors in his hands and couldn't no train throw him off and couldn't nobody turn him round. They were big enough for motors, his hands were. He held that one hand out all still and it gettin to be not at all a hand but a person in itself.

"He wants you to hand him the camera," Smilin whispers to Camera, tiltin his head to talk secret like they was in the jungle or somethin and come upon a native that don't speak the language. The men start untyin the straps, and they put the camera into that great hand speckled with the hawk's blood all black and crackly now. And the hand don't even drop with the weight, just the fingers move, curl up around the machine. But Granddaddy lookin straight at the men. They lookin at each other and everywhere but at Granddaddy's face.

"We filmin for the county, see," say Smilin. "We puttin

together a movie for the food stamp program . . . filmin all around these parts. Uhh, filmin for the county."

"Can I have my camera back?" say the tall man with no machine on his shoulder, but still keepin it high like the camera was still there or needed to be. "Please, sir."

Then Grandaddy's other hand flies up like a sudden and gentle bird, slaps down fast on top of the camera and lifts off half like it was a calabash cut for sharing.

"Hey," Camera jumps forward. He gathers up the parts into his chest and everything unrollin and fallin all over. "Whatcha tryin to do? You'll ruin the film." He looks down into his chest of metal reels and things like he's protectin a kitten from the cold.

"You standin in the misses' flower bed," say Grandaddy. "This is our own place."

The two men look at him, then at each other, then back at the mess in the camera man's chest, and they just back off. One sayin over and over all the way down to the meadow, "Watch it, Bruno. Keep ya fingers off the film." Then Grandaddy picks up the hammer and jams it into the oilskin pocket, scrapes his boots, and goes into the house. And you can hear the squish of his boots headin through the house. And you can see the funny shadow he throws from the parlor window onto the ground by the string-bean patch. The hammer draggin the pocket of the oilskin out so Granddaddy looked even wider. Granny was hummin now—high, not low and grumbly. And she was doin the cakes again, you could smell the molasses from the rum.

"There's this story I'm goin to write one day," say Cathy dreamer. "About the proper use of the hammer."

"Can I be in it?" Tyrone say with his hand up like it was a matter of first come, first served.

"Perhaps," say Cathy, climbin onto the tire to pump us up. "If you there and ready."

Basement

WHEN PATSY MOTHER TOLE ME TO DO SOMETHIN, I did it. Cause she looked like Miss Anna May Wong. The hair mostly, them bangs. And she wore shiny blouses with long smooth sleeves and stand-up collars. And if there was one thing I'd learned, it was don't mess with Miss Anna May Wong, cause somethin bad can happen to you. Like if she was the hostess in the casino and pulled your coat to bet no more, you'd be a fool to go against this sound advice and wind up with the bad guys jumpin you about them I.O.U.'s. Or like the time she was a hostess at the mysterious Grand Hotel and slipped a note in the towel for you to clear out and use the backstairs. Well, you just don't stop to shave and ring room service for ginger ale, you move. Or say she's the hostess at the waterfront club and tips you that the big guy's layin for you and there's a boat sailin at midnight. Quite naturally you get on the pier and flag that boat. Or maybe you some big-time pinky-ring gangster played by Akim Tamiroff with a ferocious make-up job around the eyes, and Miss Anna May Wong been your hostess for years and keeping a watch out for you. But this time you've fallen for a swell society dish and Miss Anna May Wong tell you to dig on yourself. And you need to check out what she saying cause never mind your big

estate and the carpets and your rings and playin Mozart
without lookin at the keyboard, you still a no-class Akim
Tamiroff and need to listen what she sayin about your life.
The swell society dish got eyes for somebody else anyway,
some bright young promising man in a tuxedo with rosy
make-up on his cheeks, cheerful stuff not like that grim mas-
cara job they stuck you with on account of you a gangster
with a foreign accent, and short besides. Not only that, Lloyd
Nolan's on your trail, so you better listen. Cause next thing
you know Miss Anna May Wong got this sweet record on the
Victrola and wearing this long shiny white gown and she
hands you a champagne glass, and, honey, it's all over. Not
that she'd poison you. Worse. She gonna speak on your life
and drop the truth in your lap. So real quiet and super-
patient, the record playin out and the camera crowdin in on
her face, she reveals how disappointed she is with you and
your dumb self. And you realize you blew, but too late. Lloyd
Nolan kickin in the door. But there she is, gorgeous for the
occasion, so your life at its end will have good taste, though
it has for a long time lacked good sense.

So when Patsy Mother tole me to stay out the basement,
I stayed out the basement. I'd throw the garbage from the
elevator without gettin out, pull the door to, quick, pressing
on the up button all the while. Or I'd stack the newspapers
on the roof. Or set the bags on the fire escape. Or fling stuff
out back. Or ride the can up and down on the elevator without me till somebody'd empty it and come to the door and
tell my mother. And she'd give me this soft-spoken lecture
about how the ironing cord was manufactured special for
certain behinds which shall remain nameless. But it didn't
come to that. Wouldn't've cared if it had. Beats gettin caught
in the spooky basement any day. I mean, you could get
yanked into the bedsprings or stuck into them bicycles and
never escape. Or get dragged down into the coal chute
where the rats with the bubonic plague would get you after

they finish tearin cats' ears off and chompin dog tails and finishin off milky-mouth babies for dessert. You might fall into the swamp there by the furnace and wouldn't no one even notice the bubbles as you got dragged under or even recognize your hat floatin on top. And if you crawled out, there's always the deadly gas leakin out the pipes, green and slimy behind the furnace, to smother you. That's if you didn't already get wound up in the lamp cords and spider nets and choke to death. And what about them crawly things in the big dirty burlap bag hangin up by the yard door? They'd snatch you up on that giant hook and you'd hang your own self. And the snow banked up gainst the yard door so you couldn't shut out the wind makin them creepy noises, cause snow don't melt in the dungeon-dark of the basement like it do in regular-type places. So, the wind'd make you run and you'd quite naturally get locked in behind the laundry room and all them whispers and roarins and scratchins give you a heart attack sure. And if you gasped still, havin survived all these goins on, then somethin fierce and hairy'd grab you by your braids and stuff you into the rag bin in the blackened brick of the wall smeared with your own sticky blood, which is smelly so the witches're howlin for your corpse for the stew pot. And you try to escape and get sunk up to your head in the quicksand by the old dumbwaiter and get dragged down past darkness till there's nothin else.

Actually, it was some time fore I got around to asking Patsy Mother just how come exactly I should stay out the basement. But she was mainly talkin with Patsy Aunt, grown-up and arguin. Me and Patsy were takin turns dressin up in the foxtails. Patsy Aunt in the yellow chair with her legs danglin over one arm of it, and her head over the other, puffin on a cigarette and sippin this highball. My mother woulda killed me. Patsy Mother in a green kimono with a gold dragon windin right around to her behind. She curlin her hair in the bathroom but comin in where we are to speak her speak, then goin out again to where the sterno and the mirror and everything else was.

"He oughta be strung up by the short hairs," was what she said in the doorway, catchin the lump of grease sliding off her wrist. "Messin with young girls with his raunchy ole diseased self," was what she mumbled back in the bathroom.

"Oh, Norma, you're always ready to believe the worst about any man. Who told you he got the Norton girl pg?"

"And another thing," comin from the bathroom fast, this time swingin the curlin iron so they click-clicked and curled their own smoke, "don't let my attitude about men be more important than these little girls' safety. You know for a fact, Fay, that you mainly stay in hot water cause you always try to prove I'm wrong about some man." And then, "Look here," as she went away, then came back, holdin the iron still and tight like that would hold the heat in for one more curl, "I like men, always did."

"Like hell. You give em as rough a time as your mouth can muster. If you could shut up for half a second and give a man a chance to . . ."

"If one kissable man would bite my tongue," said Patsy Mother real slow, "I'd be silent for days to come." She said it real clear and serious like somethin important was being put down. Like the old folks clear their throat, hold the rocker silent, and wait till the airplane go over and then lay the wise word on you. "That's the truth," she said, pointin the curlin iron straight at me and Patsy like we said different. "Men are wonderful-type persons," she said. "And if you can find one, just one man in life that knows what the hell he doing, can maybe find his own socks, and don't be bucklin at the knees or hittin you in the head or chasin around, just one man who halfway know who he dealin with and ain't too ugly to climb into bed with, don't look like he been hit in the head with a hammer, often, and enjoyed it . . ."

"See how you do, Norma," said Patsy Aunt, climbin out

the yellow chair and real careful with the highball. "You open your mouth and out it spews. Patsy'll grow up with all the wrong ideas about . . ."

"Old ugly man," Patsy Mother motioned toward the window and the yard as she headed for the bathroom, but comes back fore she get there. "Look just like a sick frog, don't he? And think he cute is the worst part."

"Well, Norma, just remember that every frog is likely to be Prince Charming himself under a spell." Me and Patsy giggle with her, but Patsy Mother squint hard and point a sharp finger to hush.

"I leave toads strictly alone," she said. "Likely to give you all kinds of warts. I leave em alone. See you do the same."

"Yes ma'am," I said. "So why must we stay out the basement?" I asked again while my mouth was open. Patsy Aunt come sit with us by the mirror and bury her face in the fox fur and giggle. Patsy Mother stare hard at the fox head around my shoulders like she waitin for them yellow eyes to blink.

"Cause the super and his cronies is a nasty bunch of low life, filthy bad, jive ass . . ."

"Because," said Patsy Aunt drownin her out, "some men when they get to drinking don't know how to behave properly to women and girls. Understand?" Me and Patsy nodded and got to brushin the foxes with the silver hairbrush from the World's Fair.

"You see," said Patsy Mother back again and with only one slipper, "it's very hard to teach young girls to be careful and the same time to not scare you to death." She came and sat down on the rug with us. "Sex is not a bad thing. But sometimes it's a need that makes men act bad, take advantage of little girls who are friendly and trusting. Understand?"

We understood, but we didn't nod in the mirror at her cause she wasn't lookin. She was busy plasterin down them bangs and kinda starin into empty glass. Patsy Aunt take the brush and brush my hair and it feel good till she get to the kitchen. "They play checkers in the basement," I said, just to get out the trance and get her out the knots. Don't nobody say nuthin. And I get to thinkin about the super who I thought was O.K. before, because he smelled like bubble gum all the time. His clothes did. I figured he smuggled bubble gum into the country past the ration board in the linin of his clothes. Smuggled it in for little kids cause it wasn't our fault about the war and why we gotta do without bubble gum just cause they need the rubber for the jeep tires. But then come to find that smell was not bubble gum but some purple tablets you suck on for your breath when you been drinkin. And I had to change my whole picture of him. So I didn't like him for that. Plus he used to pee up against the wall when we played handball. So he was definitely on my list.

"The super pulled his thing out," Patsy said after while.

"Say what?"

"He always do that."

"Tell me that again," said Patsy Mother turnin her full around from the mirror. "And don't leave nuthin out."

"Your temperature's rising, Norma."

"You shut up, Fay, and let the child speak. So?"

"I was jumpin in the yard . . ."

"After I tole you to stay your behind out the basement?"

"Let the child speak, Norma," say Patsy Aunt with that highball.

"And the super come to the doorway—the one with the dirty snow up against it—and he got on these overalls with the straps real loose so they drooped low. And he put his hand in the side like he reachin for his pocket, and he pulled his thing out."

"And what else?"

"Mighty talented man, the super. His thing reach . . ." Patsy Aunt got a look and shut up.

"He just did that. He waved it at me and Ludie and Charlane."

"What'd you do?"

"I went on jumpin. It was my turn."

"How come you didn't tell me this part when you told me about the time he felt up Cora's little girl?"

Patsy shrugged, then shrugged two more times. Patsy Mother wasn't there to see. She was up and runnin and cursin and bangin doors and Patsy Aunt scramble up after her and set her highball on the coffee table. And we could hear them scufflin in the hallway and the door slammin and Patsy Mother tear past us to the silverware drawer and I'm scared cause I'm not supposed to even be in Patsy's house and now the cops'll be here sure. Patsy scared too, cause she always makin up stuff on top of the real stuff.

"I'll kill that black bastard," Patsy Mother screamin and Patsy Aunt tryin to tackle her and wrench her coat off. Patsy hide her face in the foxtails and I can't see if she cryin or laughin or what. And I'm thinkin bout the time we almost weren't friends no more cause she told my mother I was under the stairs with James Lee. And my mother said to stay out of Patsy way cause she sex crazy and always talkin nasty. But I'm mostly thinkin I better go home before Patsy Aunt give up tryin to step on the back of Patsy Mother one houseshoe, who is crazy now to get out the door and to the super with the ice pick. But I don't move cause doorways are dangerous when them two scufflin. Like the time Patsy Mother decided somebody up the block needed cuttin cause her number hit and they disappeared and Patsy Aunt wound up gettin the dresser slammed on her hand, then her face slammed into the police lock.

"He didn't really shake his thing at you, did he?" I say

when Patsy come up out the fur to see who's winnin. Patsy don't answer. Then her mother yank herself free and out the door and Patsy Aunt pick herself up and yell down the stairs that she hope the super hit her in her head, rape her in the snow, and strangle her with her own brassiere. And I know my mother gotta be hearin this cause she home from work and always wonderin where I am is listenin out. Then we hear Patsy Aunt jumpin two at a time and yellin to Mr. Taylor who getting his mail from the hall table to do somethin. And you can't even hear his answers cause he speak proper-like and soft like my mother. So Patsy Aunt callin him a bunch of choice faggots. And I can just see my mother puttin on that camel-hair coat and reachin for her keys off the bookcase, comin to look for me. Then we hear the basement gate rattlin like maybe she climbin over or tearin it off the hinges one, so we go to the window. And the super standin there yankin on his suspenders, then backin into the snow with his hands up and there's Patsy Mother swingin on him with that one houseshoe and I'm hopin she dropped the ice pick on the way.

Cause I know how she feel about evil folks. She speak on it every time she got a highball in her hand. Like the time she set me in her lap to explain it to me and all the while her relatives jumpin up and down sayin she crazy. And she's tellin me that there is evil in the world and evil scars and tears your soul. And if you hand God a raggedy soul he don't appreciate it much, cause it may not be in shape to give out to the next person waitin to come on in. So when you murder evil, you doin good twice over. You savin your soul for you and the unborn as well. So it's not murder at all, it's fittin, is how she was tellin me till Patsy Uncle Washburn snatch me up on his shoulder and take all us down to Thomford's for raisin-rum ice-cream cones, showin us all the dance steps him and Bojangles and the man in Father Divine barbershop taught to Fred Astaire, who not only not grateful but not doin the steps right, steppin when he should glide and stompin when he should tap and havin to depend on a bouncin cane stead of his talents.

"Here, hold this," Patsy say, handing me the foxtails so she can get the nail out the window so we can really get out and see what's doing. Patsy Mother beatin hell out the super is what's doin. We see his stockin cap sailin in the air, though we can't see him cause the window nailed permanent. Besides I gotta go fore my mother come lookin for me.

"Was he feelin Rosie's tits for real that time, Patsy?"

And Patsy give me a look and suck her teeth and grab the foxtails back around her face, scrapin my neck with the claws so I get mad and gotta go anyway.

"I'm not gonna be your friend any more," I said, and got up to get my coat.

"I'll tell you a secret," she said, pulling at my sleeve. "About the time me and James Lee did it on the roof."

"You always tellin tales on people."

She ran to the door behind me and tried to snatch my hat but it buckles. "If you stay I'll show you a surprise."

"What?"

Patsy stood there tryin to figure out what in the world she had for show. She spun around on her heels looking the house over for surprisin things. But I got my gloves on now and the door open and busy trying to get a story together for my mother when she ask where I been all day. Then decide to just tell her the truth and take the weight and let it go.

But I'll leave out the part about how Patsy pulled her drawers down and her dress up and put her hand there, callin that a surprise. Some surprise. And just to make me stay and play with her and be her friend. Left out that part cause my mother don't think much of Patsy and her family as it is.

Maggie of the Green Bottles

*M*AGGIE HAD NOT INTENDED to get sucked in on this thing, sleeping straight through the christening, steering clear of the punch bowl, and refusing to dress for company. But when she glanced over my grandfather's shoulder and saw "Aspire, Enspire, Perspire" scrawled across the first page in that hard-core Protestant hand, and a grease stain from the fried chicken too, something snapped in her head. She snatched up the book and retired rapidly to her room, locked my mother out, and explained through the door that my mother was a fool to encourage a lot of misspelled nonsense from Mr. Tyler's kin, and an even bigger fool for having married the monster in the first place.

I imagine that Maggie sat at her great oak desk, rolled the lace cuffs gently back, and dipped her quill into the lavender ink pot with all the ceremony due the Emancipation Proclamation, which was, after all, exactly what she was drafting. Writing to me, she explained, was serious business, for she felt called upon to liberate me from all historical and genealogical connections except the most divine. In short, the family was a disgrace, degrading Maggie's and my capacity for wings, as they say. I can only say that Maggie was truly inspired. And she probably ruined my life from the get-go.

There is a photo of the two of us on the second page. There's Maggie in Minnie Mouse shoes and a long polka-dot affair with her stockings rolled up at the shins, looking like muffins. There's me with nothing much at all on, in her arms, and looking almost like a normal, mortal, everyday-type baby —raw, wrinkled, ugly. Except that it must be clearly understood straightaway that I sprang into the world full wise and invulnerable and gorgeous like a goddess. Behind us is the player piano with the spooky keys. And behind that, the window outlining Maggie's crosshatched face and looking out over the yard, overgrown even then, where later I lay lost in the high grass, never hoping to be found till Maggie picked me up into her hair and told me all about the earth's moons.

Once just a raggedy thing holding telegrams from well-wishers, the book was pleasant reading on those rainy days when I didn't risk rusting my skates, or maybe just wasn't up to trailing up and down the city streets with the kids, preferring to study Maggie's drawings and try to grab hold of the fearsome machinery which turned the planets and coursed the stars and told me in no uncertain terms that as an Aries babe I was obligated to carry on the work of other Aries greats from Alexander right on down to anyone you care to mention. I could go on to relate all the wise-alecky responses I gave to Maggie's document as an older child rummaging in the trunks among the canceled checks and old sheet music, looking for some suspicioned love letters or some small proof that my mother had once had romance in her life, and finding instead the raggedy little book I thought was just a raggedy little book. But it is much too easy to smile at one's ignorant youth just to flatter one's present wisdom, but I digress.

Because, on my birthday, Saturn was sitting on its ass and

Mars was taken unawares, getting bumped by Jupiter's flunkies, I would not be into my own till well past twenty. But according to the cards, and my palm line bore it out, the hangman would spare me till well into my hundredth year. So all in all, the tea leaves having had their say and the coffee-ground patterns being what they were, I was destined for greatness. She assured me. And I was certain of my success, as I was certain that my parents were not my parents, that I was descended, anointed and ready to gobble up the world from urgent, noble Olympiads.

I am told by those who knew her, whose memories consist of something more substantial than a frantic gray lady who poured coffee into her saucer, that Margaret Cooper Williams wanted something she could not have. And it was the sorrow of her life that all her children and theirs and theirs were uncooperative—worse, squeamish. Too busy taking in laundry, buckling at the knees, putting their faith in Jesus, mute and sullen in their sorrow, too squeamish to band together and take the world by storm, make history, or even to appreciate the calling of Maggie the Ram, or the Aries that came after. Other things they told me too, things I put aside to learn later though I always knew, perhaps, but never quite wanted to, the way you hold your breath and steady yourself to the knowledge secretly, but never let yourself understand. They called her crazy.

It is to Maggie's guts that I bow forehead to the floor and kiss her hand, because she'd tackle the lot of them right there in the yard, blood kin or by marriage, and neighbors or no. And anybody who'd stand up to my father, gross Neanderthal that he was, simply had to be some kind of weird combination of David, Aries, and lunatic. It began with the cooking usually, especially the pots of things Maggie concocted. Witchcraft, he called it. Home cooking, she'd counter. Then he'd come over to the stove, lift a lid with an incredible face, and comment about cesspools and fertilizers. But she'd re-

mind him of his favorite dish, chitlins, addressing the bread
box, though. He'd turn up the radio and make some remark
about good church music and her crazy voodoo records.
Then she'd tell the curtains that some men, who put magic
down with nothing to replace it and nothing much to recom-
mend them in the first place but their magic wand, lived a
runabout life, practicing black magic on other men's wives.
Then he'd say something about freeloading relatives and
dancing to the piper's tune. And she'd whisper to the kettles
that there wasn't no sense in begging from a beggar. Depending on how large an audience they drew, this could go
on for hours until my father would cock his head to the side,
listening, and then try to make his getaway.

"Ain't nobody calling you, Mr. Tyler, cause don't nobody
want you." And I'd feel kind of bad about my father like I do
about the wolf man and the phantom of the opera. Monsters,
you know, more than anybody else, need your pity cause
they need beauty and love so bad.

One day, right about the time Maggie would say something painful that made him bring up freeloaders and piper's
tunes, he began to sputter so bad it made me want to cry. But
Maggie put the big wooden spoon down and whistled for
Mister T—at least that's what Maggie and my grandmother,
before she died, insisted on calling him. The dog, always
hungry, came bounding through the screen door, stopped on
a dime by the sink, and slinked over to Maggie's legs the way
beat-up dogs can do, their tails all confused as to just what to
do, their eyes unblinkingly watchful. Maggie offered him
something from the pot. And when Mister T had finished, he
licked Maggie's hand. She began to cackle. And then, before
I could even put my milk down, up went Maggie's palm, and
bam, Mister T went skidding across the linoleum and banged
all the seltzer bottles down.

"Damn-fool mutt," said Maggie to her wooden spoon,

"too dumb to even know you're supposed to bite the hand that feeds you."

My father threw his hand back and yelled for my mother to drop whatever she was doing, which was standing in the doorway shaking her head, and pack up the old lady's things posthaste. Maggie went right on laughing and talking to the spoon. And Mister T slinked over to the table so Baby Jason could pet him. And then it was name-calling time. And again I must genuflect and kiss her ring, because my father was no slouch when it came to names. He could malign your mother and work your father's lineage over in one short breath, describing in absolute detail all the incredible alliances made between your ancestors and all sorts of weird creatures. But Maggie had him beat there too, old lady in lace talking to spoons or no.

My mother came in weary and worn and gave me a nod. I slid my peanut-butter sandwich off the icebox, grabbed Baby Jason by his harness, and dragged him into our room, where I was supposed to read to him real loud. But I listened, I always listened to my mother's footfalls on the porch to the gravel path and down the hard mud road to the woodshed. Then I could give my attention to the kitchen, for "Goldilocks," keep in mind, never was enough to keep the brain alive. Then, right in the middle of some fierce curse or other, my father did this unbelievable thing. He stomped right into Maggie's room—that sanctuary of heaven charts and incense pots and dream books and magic stuffs. Only Jason, hiding from an August storm, had ever been allowed in there, and that was on his knees crawling. But in he stomped all big and bad like some terrible giant, this man whom Grandma Williams used to say was just the sort of size man put on this earth for the " 'spress purpose of clubbing us all to death." And he came out with these green bottles, one in each hand, snorting and laughing at the same time. And I figured, peeping into the kitchen, that these bottles were enchanted, for they had a strange effect on Maggie, she shut right up. They had a strange effect on me too, gleaming there up in the air, nearly touching the ceiling, glinting off the shots of sunshine, grasped in the giant's fist. I was awed.

Whenever I saw them piled in the garbage out back I was tempted to touch them and make a wish, knowing all the while that the charm was all used up and that that was why they were in the garbage in the first place. But there was no doubt that they were special. And whenever Baby Jason managed to drag one out from under the bed, there was much whispering and shuffling on my mother's part. And when Sweet Basil, the grocer's boy, delivered these green bottles to Maggie, it was all hush-hush and backdoor and in the corner dealings, slipping it in and out of innumerable paper bags, holding it up to the light, then off she'd run to her room and be gone for hours, days sometimes, and when she did appear, looking mysterious and in a trance, her face all full of shadows. And she'd sit at the sideboard with that famous cup from the World's Fair, pouring coffee into the saucer and blowing on it very carefully, nodding and humming and swirling the grinds. She called me over once to look at the grinds.

"What does this look like, Peaches?"

"Looks like a star with a piece out of it."

"Hmm," she mumbled, and swirled again. "And now?"

Me peering into the cup and lost for words. "Looks like a face that lost its eyes."

"Hmm," again, as she thrust the cup right under my nose, and me wishing it was a box of falling glass I could look at where I knew what was what instead of looking into the bottom of a fat yellow cup at what looked like nothing but coffee grinds.

"Looks like a mouth losing its breath, Great Granny."

"Let's not get too outrageous, Peaches. This is serious business."

"Yes ma'am." Peering again and trying to be worthy of Alexander and the Ram and all my other forebears. "What it really seems to be"—stalling for time and praying for inspiration—"is an upside-down bird, dead on its back with his heart chopped out and the hole bleeding."

She flicked my hand away when I tried to point the picture out which by now I was beginning to believe. "Go play somewhere, girl," she said. She was mad. "And quit calling me Granny."

"What happened here today?" my mother kept asking all evening, thumping out the fragrant dough and wringing the dishtowel, which was supposed to help the dough rise, wringing it to pieces. I couldn't remember anything particular, following her gaze to Maggie's door. "Was Sweet Basil here this afternoon?" Couldn't remember that either, but tried to show I was her daughter by staring hard at the closed door too. "Was Great Granny up and around at all today?" My memory failed me there too. "You ain't got much memory to speak of at all, do you?" said my father. I hung onto my mother's apron and helped her wring the dishtowel to pieces.

They told me she was very sick, so I had to drag Baby Jason out to the high grass and play with him. It was a hot day and the smell of the kerosene soaking the weeds that were stubborn about dying made my eyes tear. I was face down in the grass just listening, waiting for the afternoon siren which last year I thought was Judgment Day because it blew so long to say that the war was over and that we didn't have to eat Spam any more and that there was a circus coming and a parade and Uncle Bubba too, but with only one leg to show for it all. Maggie came into the yard with her basket of vegetables. She sat down at the edge of the gravel path and began stringing the peppers, red and green, red and green. And, like always, she was humming one of those weird songs of hers which always made her seem holier and blacker than she could've been. I tied Baby Jason to a tree so he wouldn't crawl into her lap, which always annoyed her. Maggie didn't like baby boys, or any kind of boys I'm thinking, but especially baby boys born in Cancer and Pisces or anything but in Aries.

"Look here, Peaches," she called, working the twine through the peppers and dropping her voice real low. "I want you to do this thing for your Great Granny."

"What must I do?" I waited a long time till I almost thought she'd fallen asleep, her head rolling around on her chest and her hands fumbling with the slippery peppers, ripping them.

"I want you to go to my room and pull out the big pink box from under the bed." She looked around and woke up a bit. "This is a secret you-and-me thing now, Peaches." I nodded and waited some more. "Open the box and you'll see a green bottle. Wrap this apron around it and tuck it under your arm like so. Then grab up the mushrooms I left on the sideboard like that's what you came for in the first place. But get yourself back here right quick." I repeated the instructions, flopped a necklace of peppers around me, and dashed into the hot and dusty house. When I got back she dumped the mushrooms into her lap, tucked the bottle under her skirt, and smiled at the poor little peppers her nervous hands had strung. They hung wet and ruined off the twine like broken-necked little animals.

I was down in the bottoms playing with the state-farm kids when Uncle Bubba came sliding down the sand pile on his one good leg. Jason was already in the station wagon hanging onto my old doll. We stayed at Aunt Min's till my father came to get us in the pickup. Everybody was in the kitchen dividing up Maggie's things. The linen chest went to

Aunt Thelma. And the souvenirs from Maggie's honeymoons went to the freckle-faced cousins from town. The clothes were packed for the church. And Reverend Elson was directing the pianist's carrying from the kitchen window. The scattered sopranos, who never ever seemed to get together on their high notes or on their visits like this, were making my mother drink tea and kept nodding at me, saying she was sitting in the mourner's seat, which was just like all the other chairs in the set; same as the amen corner was no better or any less dusty than the rest of the church and not even a corner. Then Reverend Elson turned to say that no matter how crazy she'd been, no matter how hateful she'd acted toward the church in general and him in particular, no matter how spiteful she'd behaved towards her neighbors and even her blood kin, and even though everyone was better off without her, seeing how she died as proof of her heathen character, and right there in the front yard too, with a bottle under her skirts, the sopranos joined in scattered as ever, despite all that, the Reverend Elson continued, God rest her soul, if He saw fit, that is.

The china darning egg went into Jason's overalls. And the desk went into my room. Bubba said he wanted the books for his children. And they all gave him such a look. My mother just sat in the kitchen chair called the mourner's seat and said nothing at all except that they were selling the house and moving to the city.

"Well, Peaches," my father said. "You were her special, what you want?"

"I'll take the bottles," I said.

"Let us pray," said the Reverend.

That night I sat at the desk and read the baby book for the first time. It sounded like Maggie for the world, holding me in her lap and spreading the charts on the kitchen table. I looked my new bottle collection over. There were purple bottles with glass stoppers and labels. There were squat blue bottles with squeeze tops but nothing in them. There were flat red bottles that could hold only one flower at a time. I had meant the green bottles. I was going to tell them and then I didn't. I was too small for so much enchantment anyway. I went to bed feeling much too small. And it seemed a shame that the hope of the Aries line should have to sleep with a light on still, and blame it on Jason and cry with balled fists in the eyes just like an ordinary, mortal, everyday-type baby.

The
Johnson
Girls

"DON'T BE THUMPIN THAT BALL on my shadow, boy," Great Ma Drew warn Thumb, sifting through the lentils. "Your sister tole you once to get to that paintin on the third floor, and her nerves worn thin. Mine too."

Thumb dribble past the old woman again, squeezing by me and damn near upsetting the ironing board. Great Ma Drew tip her chair back gainst the wall so her shadow scurry under her, leaving Thumb on a blank court. He stand right in my face, swirling the ball on one finger and smiling that smile. I am not impressed. Far as I am concerned Thumb a clown. Which is why when he come into my room last night talking about he looking for Inez about some turpentine and all the while bouncing around my room, touching the jars on my dresser and the books on my bed, till finally he leaning over me drawing zigzags on my leg through the cover—I say to him, "Look here, Thumb, you a very fine dude and all that, but I do not take clowns to bed so get on outta here." And quite naturally he say for the hundredth time that I'm getting more like Inez every day. And I cut him off and send him on his way. Cause Thumb the type to keep up a steady stream of chatter and never really get down to business, or if his body do then his mouth don't, rapping away about some movie he seen or some speech he heard or some book he read or some other elsewhere goings on as if he weren't in my bed trying to get his jones off without quite letting himself know it, just in case Inez ask if he been messin around with me, he can say no and be in the clear. Or in case he a total flop at love-making and I pitch him out the bed on his head, why then he a poor-mistreated man and I'm some crazy bitch.

"Stead of burning roots, you could send Roy a telegram sayin you comin," say Thumb when Inez rustle past in that taffeta slip she's had on all day, sticking the incense into the fireplace bricks.

"Was me," say Great Ma Drew, "I'd set up some counter juju and get that man turned right around again." Inez not payin neither one of them any mind, jugglin the fifty-leven lists of things in her head she's got to do fore she can fly to Knoxville and bring Roy home, or hit him in the head one.

"Whatcha got there, Nez, love charm?"

"Just keys," she says, opening her fist to show the keys and the crumpled note Roy left which we all been dying to read, but she ain't put it down in the past twenty-four hours. "Just keys," she says again to the old woman.

"Same thing, love. He give em back, hunh? Love charms are temporary things if your mojo ain't total." Inez look at the old woman so hard she shift her eyes back into the lentils, pickin the crap out with them gnarled hands. Then Inez beam them do-this-do-that eyes on her brother.

"Look now, Thumb, you supposed to be painting the upstairs rooms. And take a bath too. Incense can't cover funk too tough." She yell up after him when he dashes past, mumblin about what a cold bitch she is, to tell Sugar and them to set her makeup out and clear off the bed. Then she beaming them eyes on Great Ma Drew.

"I'ma do this floor up proper," the old lady say right quick, meaning the kitchen and dining room and pantry and fireplace.

"Look, just give the floor a quick douche, swipe at the

table with some polish and get the pots on." Then Inez back up the stairs. But time she up on the landing, talking to Sugar and them, the old lady easin herself back in the chair and spreading the cards out. She crook a finger to me to come over and study the cards with her. Jack o'diamonds is on the floor. Jack o'diamonds is always on the floor when Great Ma Drew do the cards for Inez. And I'm waitin for her to lean over and say, "Lookee there, the good man done got away" and then complain about her arthritis. Which means I'm supposed to stop pressing the nightgowns out and lean over and get the good man and spin him cross the cards to see how he settle. Maybe on the joy cards, in which case I'm supposed to race through the house, hollerin jubilee. Or maybe on the ace of sorrows, in which case I'm supposed to make an appropriate face and fix her a drink so we can commiserate about Roy never comin home again to build a fire in the fireplace and play the flute. I continue pressin is what I do and let the jack o'diamonds go for himself.

"See now, when I was comin up," she say, bammin the cards down, "the older women would gather together to train you young girls in the ways of menfolks." I yawn cause I'm sick of this speech and in a hurry to get back upstairs with Sugar and them, cause it's right about this time they'll be ordering pizza or something to tide them over till Great Ma Drew can get the supper together. "And you learn what to do when mens get raffish or start gazin too long a spell into empty space. And you learn about charms and things and how to read the signs so . . ."

"You wanna get me another bowl of water so I can do these lace numbers?"

"I do not," she say, which is O.K. by me, long as she shuttin up about that particular shit. But soon's I fold the lace jobs and reachin for the red see-through, here she go again. "You ain't but a teen-ager and think you grown cause you in college and got a story in some magazine and had some silly boys in your bed, but you unprepared. Young gal like you out there in the wilderness with no proper training, like a babe going into a dynamite shaft."

"A what? You been drinking that furniture polish again?"

"A dynamite shaft, I said. All boarded up on the outside and ready to blow. And only shaky beams holding the rocks up off your head and splinterin fast fast and the tunnel way so dark and bumpy you couldn't find your way outta there even if you had the best flashlight that money . . ."

"Hey look here, my sweet," I say, snatchin up the gowns for the getaway, "put up the ironin board for me will ya, O.K.? Gotta run. You're a dear."

"Kiss my ass," she say, and sweeps the jack o'diamonds up off the floor, neat, smooth, unarthritic.

"You ain't taking these drawers to Knoxville," say Sugar, holding up some blue cotton panties with white polka dots. "Oh no, sister, I ain't lettin you pack this draggy number."

Inez don't even turn around. Not that there's any room to turn around in. Marcy in the closets, the doors folded completely open, snatching sweaters every which way till she find somethin suitable to pack, then she fling it over on the bed. Gail crawling all over the bed, her behind all up in the air and the tops of the pantyhose showing. She matchin up tops and bottoms—velvet bells this and cableknit that. Sugar, at the chest of drawers Roy'd built in under the bay window. She damn near yanking the hardware off and rummaging through the lingerie like she got a tip money hidden somewhere. I just stand there for a second, cause it's a funny sight.

"What about this?" Marcy ask, and everybody freeze, screwin up they face to see if the red crochet dress is saying anything. Everybody but Inez. She's very methodically packin her douche bag, pills, deodorant and stuff into a plastic case. And I'm wondering why they all bothered to come over

166

and tear up the place like this when number two, the bag
Inez got sitting on the bench is so damn small, and number
one, she pack what she gonna pack and later for all of them
anyway.

"Leave the door open, sweetheart," Sugar say to me.
"Don't want to miss the bell."

"Whatshisname picking you up here, Sugar?" Gail say.
"I don't know what you see in that ugly old man. Got no
dough and no politics neither." Sugar just look at Gail and
they all bust out laughing. "That cat in the suede hat you
had with you at Marcy's opening was fine. Whatcha want
with Whatshisname is beyond my brain." Sugar give Gail
that same look and they fall out again. "Now seems to me
Leon would catch your eye. He thinks you shit diamonds
and pee Chanel Number Five, the way he knocks himself
out every time you ask him to do something. Ain't too
heavy in the mind department, but he looks as though he
might be able to keep up with his own socks and fix a
leaky faucet or something."

"I love a handy man," sigh Marcy, posing in the closet
like she'd grown up worshippin toolboxes and hacksaws
and shit, dream-walking through lumberyards questing
the plumber prince or something. We just look at her,
Marcy Stevens, sculptress in a trance, leaning against
Inez's shoerack with a long velour purple knit tunic up
against her like it was the fairy-princess gown. Then the
bell rings and it's the man with the heroes, and Sugar
with her plump self scoots back with the piles of stuff they
all fall on so fast, all I get is two plastic cups of cole slaw
and half a hero, mostly sauce and onions.

"One day," say Sugar, lickin the tomato sauce off her
arm, "what I want's goin to be on the menu. Served up to
my taste and all on one plate, so I don't have to clutter up
the whole damn table with a teensy bowl of this and a
plate of extra that and a side order of what the hell." She

shimmy her buns on top of the dresser and plants her feet in the bottom drawer. "Cause let Sister Sugar hip you bitches, living à la carte is a trip."

"Tell it all, Sister Sugar," say Gail.

"First, you gotta have you a fuckin man, a cat that can get down between the sheets without a whole lotta bullshit about 'This is a spiritual union' or 'Women are always rippin off my body' or . . ."

"Amen," say Marcy.

"Course, he usually look like hell and got no I.Q. atall," say Sugar. "So you gots to have you a go-around man, a dude that can put in a good appearance so you won't be shame to take him round your friends, case he insist on opening his big mouth." Inez laugh her first laugh of the day and lean back in the chair to do her nails.

"Course, the go-round man ain't about you, he about his rap and his wardrobe and his imported deodorant stick with the foreign ingredients listed there at the bottom in some unknown tongue. Which means you gots to have a gofor."

"A gopher?" I ask, and they all look me over carefully to make sure I am finally old enough for these big-league sessions.

"Like when you crazy with pain and totally messed around and won't nobody on earth go for your shit, you send for the gofor cause he go for it whatever it is."

"Rah-rah for the gofors," say Marcy, flapping a sea-green paisley vest in the air.

"You gots to have your money man, that goes without saying. And more importantly, you got to have you a tender man."

"I loves me a tender man," sigh Marcy, who's beginning to sound fickle to me cause she sighin just as sexy as she did for the handyman dude.

"A tender man who can tend to your tenderest needs. Maybe it means painting your bedroom a dumb shade of orange, cause just so happens you need that dumb shade of orange in your life right now. Or holding your head while you heave your insides into the toilet on account you been tryin to drown some jive ass sucker in alcohol, and knowin all the while it won't wash."

"Speak on it, Dame Sugar," say Gail.

"Or maybe it's just spoon-feeding you and putting on your pink angora socks and rubbin your tired feet while you launch into some sad-ass saga about peeing in your pants in the second grade and how that set you on the wrong course of life forever after and . . ."

"He's beginning to sound like the gopher," I say, and then I'm sorry. Cause they all lookin at me, even Inez with her left hand rotating and glistening red, like I am indeed that pitiful babe stumblin into Great Ma Drew's dynamite shaft without a candle to my name.

"Oh but honey," Sugar say, shoveling in the green peppers, "one day I'm gonna have it all and right on the same plate. Cause à la carte is a bitch."

"Being a together woman is a bitch," say Marcy.

"Being a bitch is a bitch," say Gail.

"Men a bitch," is my two cents, which seems to get over.

"But one day my prince will come," sings Marcy, waltzing around with Inez's black sequined sweater. Sugar look at her like she crazy. Inez smile that slow smile. But Gail get up off the bed for a closer look at the hole in Marcy head.

"Prince? You waiting for a prince? That's anti-struggle, sister," say Gail and they all crack, "counter-revolutionary and just plain foolish. Princes do not come. Frogs come. And they are never the enchanted kind. And they are definitely not about some magic kiss. They give you warts, sister."

"That's right," say Sugar, jumping down from the dresser and poking up her belly and swellin up her cheeks till I thought I'd die.

"It's either à la carte or half a loaf," Inez say real serious,

which is her way. Then she's messin around in the manicure
basket for the cotton and not sayin nuthin. And it's grim and
sober there for a minute. Marcy quiet in the closet, selecting
shoes. Gail making piles of hot pants. Sugar back on the
dresser top, devourin a pickled pepper very quietly. Everybody thinking the same thing, but Inez won't speak on it,
cause that's her way too, silent. And after living with cousin
Inez for three years, I still can't get used to it. Then it's real
quiet. And you can hear Thumb upstairs banging cans
around and Great Ma Drew downstairs hummin. And it always winds up to a moment like this when there's some big
thing in Inez's life and all her friends gather, mostly the
in-group. And everybody lays out their program, most times
movin on incomplete information cause Inez don't give up
much, so they make up whatever's missing and then ex-
change advice and yell at each other's stupidities and trade
stories and finally lay the consensus thing to be done on Inez.
Who turns right around and does exactly what she's going to
do in the first damn place, cause that too is her way. Like
hauling me out of my grandmother's house to come live with
her and then telling Sugar to cough up my school expenses
and find me a job, when it was mainly Sugar who said to leave
my ass where it was. Or like buyin this brownstone and hiring
Great Ma Drew as housekeeper, when as any fool can see she
can't hardly keep care of her own damn self, much less a
four-story house. Or like quitting a good paying job in pub-
lishing to set up the jazz academy so Roy wouldn't have to
go on the road so much. Or like havin Roy move in and then
refusin to marry him. And Sugar goin into a marvelous break-
down screamin, "You gotta protect your interest with a legal-
ized piece of paper, Nez." And Inez sayin "Sheeeet."

"Whatcha goin to do, Nez?" say Marcy hidin in the closet,
all big and brave. "Could be he's already accepted the teach-
ing post and found himself another woman." She say it real
quiet, swingin hangers back and forth and not showing her-

self in case Inez starts beamin them eyes. And it's a surprise to me, cause little Marcy never is the one to come right on out with stuff lessen it's her own stuff. In which case she swoons and rants and bites her knuckles and talks about how all her life she been waitin for little boys to grow up and stop pullin her braids, waitin for big boys to grow up and put down the pool sticks and come find her, young men to grow up and stop lying to each other in the locker room and come deal with her for real, men to grow up and stop saving themselves for Hollywood, or throwing themselves away on drugs, or kidding themselves with gray girls. To just grow up and stop short right in front of her and say, I'm here, Marcy Alexander Stevens. I am your man and everything gonna be alright from here on end.

"What the note say, Nez?" Marcy ask after while, but still in the closet. Inez don't answer. She's polishing her toes now. Her head tilted on the knee so that the lamp light make her fro seem grayer than it really is. "Just 'Bye bye,' or does it . . ."

"If it *is* another woman," say Gail real slow, "which it very well may be, they might be married by now. He left two weeks before you got back from lecturing. He's been down there time and time again these past few months and it don't take that much to set up a concert. Mayhap he's had a babe stashed away in Knoxville all this time. Though why anyone'd want to be in Knoxville when everything they could possibly ever want in life is right here in New York is beyond my brain."

Inez cock her head to the side and say "Thanks, Gail," very quietly, then starts in on her left foot with the polish.

"Well," said Sugar, "I never was one to put up no hue and cry over some man slipping through my chubby fingers, but that particular man of yours, Nez, is somethin special. I mean the two of you kept my faith in the blue-plate special." Sugar walk around Inez's chair then stop before the mirror to tug her suede skirt around, suckin her stomach in and winkin at herself. "It always seemed to me like . . . well, look at it," she said, heaving an arm full of air up on the suitcase like she was spreadin out maps and charts for study hour. "A man, no matter how messy he is, I mean even if he some straight-up basket case, can always get some good woman, two or three for that matter, to go for his shit. Right? But a woman? If her shit ain't together, she can forget it unless she very lucky and got a Great Ma Drew working roots. If she halfway together and very cold-blooded, then maybe she can snatch some sucker and bump his head. But if she got her johnson to-gether, is fine in her do, superbad in her work, and terrible, terrible extra plus with her woman thing, well . . ." Sugar heaved up another armful of air for examination, "she'll just bop along the waves forever with nobody to catch her up, cause her thing is so tough, and it's so crystal clear she ain't goin for bullshit, that can't no man pump up his boyish heart good enough to come deal with her one on one." Sugar flopped down on the bed beside Gail and stared at her stock-ings, exhausted. "But you and Roy," she said, shakin her head and bellowing, "Chiiiiiile. Look here. I am in the prime of my life and I am ready to cop. Do you hear me?" she said, jump-ing up.

"We hear you," say Gail.

"I am in the prime of my life and I am ready to cop. And I mean to cop. And I want it all and all on one damn plate. Am I coming through?"

"Loud and clear, Sugar," say Gail.

"And if I can't have the blue-plate special I have been readying up for these thirty-some odd years, then I'll settle for the half loaf Nez say Roy is. Any day. Any time of any day at all. Big black dude with fat thighs pushing through his slacks. Deep brown voice sayin righteous reasonable lovin things. Beautiful hands and teeth. And when he moves and them corduroys go swish swish I just holler do it do it. Do you understand?"

"You smokin," say Gail.

I'm lookin close at Sugar cause I hear the note that means she goin to cry. And when she starts that bouncin up and down on her toes, not givin a shit bout runs in her stockings or wrinkles in the suede, why then, that's a sign of rain. And it embarrasses me. Not when she cries, but later. Like at the television studio when I come meet her for lunch and she in her long leather outfit with the bad hat ace deuce and her shades and she dealin and doin and kickin ass and everybody jumpin hup-two-three cause Mrs. Elizabeth Daley born Williams called Sugar is a bad bitch and on the case and doin derrin-do. And she strolls across the carpet in them incredible boots and that cigarette holder at just-so angle and the impossible eyelashes just right and the make-up unduplicatable. And she's takin me to some fancy restaurant even if I do pick over the food, cause she says I must be exposed to the very best so can't no Nedick's nigger sweep me off my feet and set me on my ass. And she leans over to kiss me hello. And she smells good. And says I look nice in my Levi suit and that I'll get over my army-navy-surplus defiance soon and be gorgeous like she never was. And we stroll out and everybody noddin and wavin and grinnin and damn near yankin the door off the hinges and hailin a cab. Then I get embarrassed about them wet eyes of 3:00 A.M. some weeks ago. Like I'm carryin an awful secret in my pea-jacket pocket and must not pull my hand out too quick less it tumble out and sprawl on the pavement for enemy eyes, and Sugar be undone.

"Hand me some cole slaw," Sugar say to me, kickin off her shoes. And I hear in her voice that she is not goin to cry but eat herself sick instead. Gail assists her in the uncappin of the cup and the huntin for the fork like the friend she is. And I'm

173

waitin on Gail to speak. Not so much for Inez, cause Inez just don't care what's goin on in other people's heads, her program's internal. But speak for me, cause I'm keepin a notebook on all this, so I won't have all this torture and crap to go through when I jump into my woman stride and stalk out on the world. So I'm lookin to Gail.

"The other day," Gail starts off, leaning back on her elbows and pausin a bit to examine her tits which she says are her best feature "Rudi . . . the dude that used to bartend at the corner fore he got busted? . . . he comes down to the center and snatches me off for a drink, all right? Been in the slams for three years, got that? Nailed his ass knockin over a bank, but time enough to stash the bucks so his woman and kid could live comfy and keep up the payments on the house. O.K. His mama comes to the joint to report that above-mentioned woman has got a new nigger and said nigger's been spending the weekends at the house. All praises due to good-news-bearin mama, right? So the cat plots his moves. Gets out the joint in the P.M. and ain't told a soul, got the picture? Goes to house. Spies car in driveway. Notes coat and hat on sofa. Tips upstairs to bedroom and finds exactly what any fool'd expect. Well, hell, three years is three years. So. He proceeds to commit various unhospitality-type mayhem acts on the party of the first part and the party of the other parts. Much ass kicked and a little razor action thrown in for ethnic sake. Throws woman out in the snow. Whips the nigger to a fare-thee-well. Packs son off to previously cited mama." Gail uncrossed her legs, met Inez's eye for a minute, then snatched Sugar's cigarette for the windup. "Now Rudi is scrunched up against me in this red-leather booth in a downtown bar telling me all this in a heavy righteous voice and feeling my legs and figurin I'll go for it cause ain't my man in the joint doing five to seven and hey I'm dragged. Not just behind the dramatic irony, not just cause I should be in the meeting of the street workers, but mostly cause Rudi's rap is such a drag."

"What did you say?" ask Marcy.

"I raised a few questions, like one, ain't a woman human too? Two, what he expect? Three, why didn't he just do the righteous thing and say to her from jump street, 'Look, baby, three years is a long haul, so take care of whatever you need to and I'll give you plenty notice fore I come home so you can cut all the shit loose so things are squared away when I hit the door.' "

"What Rudi say?" ask Marcy, comin over and sittin on the bed.

"That fool says that if she just had to have a nigger, she shouldn't've brought him to their house, shouldn't've. Should've gone to a hotel. Dig that. He'd rather have his woman runnin in and out of hotels all over town with everyone peepin his action and have strangers in his house babysitting their son all hours of the night. Men a bitch. A natural bitch."

"Parables usually have a lesson," say Inez, not lookin up but blowin on her hands.

"Well," say Gail, "whatcha expect? A, man is philanderin by nature. B, there are simply not enough men to go around so Roy bound to get snatched. C, you refuse to train that man to stay in orbit or to lock him up at night cause you about freedom and mobility and respect and all that shit. D, your thing is pretty heavy to deal with, Inez, and most men . . . O.K., I'll give Roy his due, he's groovier and more solid than most men, but he's still a man, his mama like everybody else raised a son and left the job of polishin him off to manhood to other women, right? . . . well, he just can't stand up under the kind of pressure a sister like you lay out there."

Inez lean way back in the chair and cover her eyes like she thinkin on this pressure and maybe rejectin the motion.

175

Cause she always maintainin that she offers a tax-free relationship—no demands, no pressure, no games, no jumpin up and down with ultimatums. And it's usually Gail that spews steam at that juncture, pointing out that that is the heaviest damn pressure of all. And Inez sayin "Sheeeet" and goin on about her business.

"So," Gail continued slowly, expectin some static from that quarter, "in conclusion, it is my position that first of all you should call Roy and give him fair warning so you don't walk into nothing you gonna have to shoot your way out of. Second, that you do not take your finest threads in your good bag, but just stuff any ole shit into any ole thing packed any ole how and simply fling yourself at his knees and systematically fall apart so that Roy can . . ."

We all knew she'd never get to three. And we all knew exactly what the interrupter would be, so we all sat up straight in the bed and drowned Inez out with her own "Sheeeet." "I know," said Gail, leanin off the bed as if to shove Inez back into the chair if she was thinkin of gettin up and walkin out, "you are not about the heavy drama and intrigue. 'No guile, no guilt,' as you would say."

"I got a right to be exactly who I am," say Sugar, mimicking Inez.

"The only proper mask to wear in life is your own damn face," Marcy sayin just like Inez do it.

"But you see," say Gail, "Roy is a rare bird. Believe me. I been out there jitterbuggin since kindergarten and I know what I'm talkin about. Men? That's my best shot. And what's out there is nothing. Got that? Sheer unadulterated foul folk nuthin. And Roy requires super heavy plottin cause he's worth all the trouble that his sulky exit is causin you and your best friends. Now," Gail smoothed the wrinkles from across her thighs and stood up. "Here we are," she said, giving a grand sweep to take us all in, "the Johnson girls. Seems to me we can certainly come up with a sure-fire program to get you over, Inez, whatever it is you want. Not just to grab him outta Knoxville and run fifty yards. But a total program."

Gail walked over to the suitcase and swept her hand across it like Sugar's maps and charts were being thrown aside for the master plan.

"We have twelve hours to plane time," she said. "Let's deal."

"I'm ready," said Sugar, scraping the chairs up like it was poker night in Dodge City. "Cause I need a Nez and Roy in my life to keep the blue-plate special on the horizon."

"I'll tell the root lady to conjure up some coffee and put a hold on dinner," said little Marcy prancing out into the hallway.

"I'll send Thumb for cigarettes," I said, certain in a sudden way that I could send Thumb for anything anywhere at any time and to Turkey for smokes if necessary. And just like some telepathic happnin, here come Thumb taking six steps at a time and smilin his smile and his eyebrows up as if to say, Can I do somethin for you, baby. So I mime a puff and he split through the door and I'm kinda diggin him as I turn back into the room.

"O.K.," said Inez like she never said before and drew her chair up to the suitcase. It halted me in my tracks and Gail looked dumbfounded. "O.K.," she said again and something caught me in my ribs. Love love love love love. We all sat down and Inez opened her fist and the keys and the crumpled note fell out on the suitcase. Sugar look at Gail and Gail look at Marcy and Marcy look at me. I look at Inez and she's sittin so forward I see the tremor caterpillar up her back. And I can't breathe. Somebody has opened a wet umbrella in my chest. And I shudder for me at the preview of things to come.

"O.K.," I say, takin command. "Let's first deal with the note."

"Right," say Gail, and lights my cigarette.